The
Void Codex

IT CREEL

IT CREEL

ISBN: 0692545476
ISBN-13: 978-0692545478 (zeplemon productions)

For Kim, Preston, Logan, and Esther.

ACKNOWLEDGMENTS

James "Tombstone" Tombe ~ Editing
Kelly Hogan ~ Editing/ Formatting
Becca Rhodes ~ Medic
Clint Simmons ~ Cover Picture
Doug Wingate ~ Cover Design

Act 1

1

The fire was still going strong, with a stack of wood piled behind the taller of the two grizzled young men laughing uproariously from their seats on the rocks directly across from mine. The heat was welcome after weeks of passing out from exhaustion and dripping rain water following our flight out of the city. Our socks were all in a row on a rock to my right, our clothes on another rock to the left, and the three of us were huddled beneath separate dingy blankets, snatched up in haste while moving from house to house. Foresight was a luxury that none of us experienced as what would be called "the Invasion" started a few days ago, so wishing for the surplus Army gear that was sitting in my garage wouldn't make it appear before me.

"Wish in one hand and shit in the other," I could hear my father's voice say, "and see which one fills up faster."

Thanks dad.

Cody and Jim...Jake...something with a "J" were keeping their own spirits up with stories of their sexual conquests--a diversion that had long since lost its thrill during my youth--while I struggled to make sense of my next moves in this whole thing. Their youth had been advantageous as we ran through the chaos that had once been our quiet Washington town, but their voices grew a little too loud for prudence. A stare from me brought them down to a reasonable level, granting me enough peace of mind to return to my brooding.

181 miles in a car would take roughly 3 hours under normal circumstances, but who knew how far the checkpoints and patrols extended beyond the Seattle Metro area. Certainly, one of the main targets had been Fort Lewis and I had little doubt that Army Strykers were being used even as I huddled and shivered around the campfire with my two recruits. They too had speculated earlier that the best option was to link up with the Army and offer their patriotism to fight the invaders who had destroyed their way of life.

I had other plans.

***

When the city of Seattle lost cell phone coverage for two hours, I sent my wife and kids to Oregon. She phoned me from her dad's house to tell me how ludicrous I was being.

"It's just a solar flare or something, remember that thing I told you about on I Fucking Love Science?"

"Yeah, you're probably right. But listen, I put the gun under the driver seat of the van, okay?"

"You what?!?"

The conversation was short but I made sure to talk to the boys, to tell them to listen very carefully to mommy and that I'd see them soon. Two hours for a city that is one of the most technologically advanced on the planet should have given the Department of Defense pause, and I'm certain that someone at the NSA was freaking out, but the ball was definitely dropped somewhere. I mentioned how odd it was to my coworkers, some of whom were veterans from different parts of the country who found themselves in the Seattle area, and they agreed it was weird but that was the extent of the speculation/ preparation.

A news report came out an hour after the incident with the official word from all the major telecoms that they were looking into the issue and that it wasn't Chinese hackers, most likely it was an atmospheric anomaly, but NASA didn't have a statement ready. All subscribers were given an upgrade in their digital data plans, and that was the end of it. My wife left after the press conference and made it to Gresham without incident, so I locked all the doors in the house, got my things ready for work the next day and crawled into bed.

***

"How about you," J-something's voice brought me back to the present. "What do you think they're going to do?"

"I don't know, probably sweep south," I mumbled, not prepared to deal with the thought that that meant eventually making their way to Portland.

"Whatever, Lewis will stop 'em."

They continued chatting softly between themselves as I provided no relevant feedback for them. I anticipated they were partially correct-- Fort Lewis would provide resistance long enough, I hoped, for me to make my way south. A part of me wanted to join my brothers-in-arms and mount a frontal attack on these devils, but just as certainly as I knew Lindsay had had to get out of there, I knew that any resistance at this point was going to be ripped apart until we knew more about our enemy. No, I had to make with all haste south, link up with my family and stay safe until someone could make headway against this insurmountable force.

I ran through routes and maps in my head until the fire started getting low and I could no longer keep my eyes open. Some small voice in my head told me to establish a watch shift, but I was exhausted once again...

***

CRASH!

I rolled out of bed and grabbed the lamp sitting on the bedside table. Another loud blast, followed by gunshots. I waited, counting seconds. One, two, three, four. Another blast, this time with sirens. Gunshots. I pulled some cargo pants on, threw a hoodie over my head, socks, and my shitty old garden boots, rushing to the window. Flashes of light every few seconds. Gunshots. Screaming now. All the sounds getting closer and closer. I ran downstairs, grabbed my bug-out bag, and ran out the back door to the woods behind my house.

Lights were popping on in the houses on my street. People rushing outside in their underwear were yelling to each other, asking what the hell was happening. Police sirens were wailing from down the street. Some of my neighbors had shotguns or hunting rifles, trying to figure out what was going on. I stayed put in the deep bushes behind my house, totally obscured but watching as the scene grew increasingly chaotic. Something brushed my leg! I looked at the face of my cat. When I looked up, I saw a flash of light at the house across the street then felt heat and a deafening roar as I dropped prone.

Debris from the house flew everywhere. Car alarms were going off and Larry from next door was hollering for his kids to get back inside. I watched as Tabitha collapsed in the street, fire engulfing her as she writhed on the concrete near her azaleas, her husband screaming and hitting at the flames with his own shirt. People were crying or hiding behind cars and orienting their weapons towards the origin of all the mess. Dogs were running out of their houses and down the street as fast as they could, away from the destruction. Beagles, Labradors, that annoying purse dog, all bolting away from their masters by the tens, now snowballing into at least fifty all running from the direction of the chaos down our street.

I took my cue from them.

***

I bolted upright quickly, scanning the area around our little camp for any source of danger. The fire was dead, but still smoking faintly, and my two companions were passed out next to each other huddled under their shabby blankets. I pulled my dry clothes off the rock and dressed quietly in the dark. They must have been in their early twenties, the kind of kids who would have snubbed me months earlier if I asked them if they were interested in a career with the Army. Right now they looked like regular grunts three weeks into a field problem. I didn't wish them harm. They were just kids after all. But I had a feeling they would get me in trouble, so I gathered my things and left while they slept there in the woods.

Maybe they will make it to Lewis, I thought half-heartedly. Maybe they'll link up with an infantry unit and fight back. They'll learn on the job, like soldiers from the old days, driven only by the desire to stop a vastly superior force with no concern for college money or health insurance. In a way, I envied them. They were driven by revenge, patriotism, and youthful fervor where I was driven entirely by hope. My family was out there, waiting for me to come back and protect them. Waiting for daddy to come home and make the monsters go away. I would not let them down.

As I made my way through the woods alone in the darkness, I

noticed just how quiet things had grown in such a short period of time. Over the last few days of traveling with the two kids, I had been annoyed by their constant jabber and disregard for noise discipline. Now I found myself quite alone in a very uncertain world. The lack of small talk wasn't everything though. There was a deeper quiet now, as if all the birds and squirrels that had inhabited these woods had vanished. I quickened my pace, stumbling through the underbrush in the predawn light, trying to be as quiet as possible with a pervasive sense of dread. Suddenly I felt the earth shake and heard a snapping of trees coming from the direction of the camp.

The rumbling of some great machine accompanied the sound of trees snapping and falling as I bolted through the woods, vines and branches scratching at my face and any exposed flesh. I heard the yells of Cody and J as they awoke and made a run for it, too, but they were cut short after another tree fell. Whatever monstrosity was pushing its way through the forest took no notice of the two humans that were caught in its path, just as surely as it would not pause over my corpse.

I flipped on my headlamp--stealth was irrelevant at the moment--and broke into a run, altering my course but maintaining a generally southern path. Adrenaline pumped steadily through my veins as sweat streamed over the open wounds on my face. I couldn't have stopped if I wanted to. Whatever I was running from didn't sound like it was making very good time. It must have been huge to crush trees like that but they were definitely slowing it down, so the advantage was with me as I struggled with ferns and nurse logs until the woods thinned out around me. Eventually, I could only hear the beast faintly behind me as the woods dropped away entirely into a small clearing with a dilapidated two-story house in its center.

A bullet turned the ground to my left into a spray of dirt that slapped my face and my cold war-era camouflage rain jacket.

"Don't you fucking move!" came a voice from the second story window. "That shot was a warning. One more step and you're dog meat!"

"You need to get the hell out of here right now, mister!" I yelled. "There's one of them behind me!"

"Bullshit! You're one of them goddamned...." His voice trailed off as a distant crack of wood from the forest brought the situation to his attention. "Don't just stand there! Get the fuck in here!"

He disappeared back into the house while I ran towards the front door. I heard footsteps, a rattling of chains, the slide of a deadbolt and the door opened. I got a good look at the guy. He was in his 60s, but looked like he could hold his own in a bar fight. He wore a flannel shirt and dirty jeans. He clutched a hunting rifle in one hand and used the other one to pull me into a dimly lit front room crowded with stacks of newspaper and books.

"Get in here!" he barked as he slammed the door shut and hurried towards the back of the house. "Sounds close. That means we don't have much time. Look, take what you can from the cupboard and fill that pack of yours." He disappeared and left me in a kitchen strewn with dirty dishes and peeling wallpaper. "Name's Zeke," he continued as he disappeared around the corner and I made my way to the cupboard.

"Pete," I muttered.

Some peanut butter, a couple cans of tuna, and a zip lock bag of some type of jerky all went into the pack. He came back around the corner with two MREs, which he threw to me. I stuffed them into my backpack as he closed the distance, pulling some small boxes out of a satchel he'd slung over his shoulder.

"Nine mil," he said, handing them to me and digging around in the bag. "Got a piece?"

"No."

"Okay, take this, too." He handed me a pistol. "Not that it'll do much good, but it's better than what you've got. Ready?"

I dropped the magazine, cleared the chamber, and replaced the magazine. "Let's go."

2

In the name of God, the merciful and just, my dreams prior to my first day of American school were so vivid that there shall be no error when I recount them here, such were the dreams granted to me by God that night, some of which have already come to pass, and some of which I should pray in His Holy Name should never befall this Earth, for if they should indeed begin here not a one amongst us who has yet to turn towards God shall be united in the glorious kingdom of heaven.

My dream began in a vast prairie, the kind which I have known from watching the old black-and-white movies my father (God rest his soul) loved so much. The kind with grass so tall that it brushes your hips as you wade through it. Such a sea of grass as to inspire the American "amber waves of grain." Indeed, the color there was the same blonde as the gorgeous Jennifer Aniston, from when I snuck into the family room late at night to watch Friends on Satellite TV back home. So inspiring was that place with the air stretching from the land upwards into infinity, a deep blue from God's brush as he dipped it into the ocean and dragged it across the canvas of the sky unto Heaven itself. No clouds to mar the perfection of His master-stroke, no sun to bake my skin as I stood beneath Heaven in a pure white dress which flowed over my shoulders and rested against the marble floor of the amphitheater on which I stood, my black hair exposed under God's protection and I, uninhibited in that perfect place!

I spun there on the stage of the marble amphitheater, a circle with a radius of nine meters surrounded by nine rows of bench-steps, soaking in the warmth and beauty of that place until from the very Earth there came a deep rumbling. The pure sheet of stone that was used in the creation of that perfect place by the Hand of God was being rent by some internal force of unknown purpose. I was frightened by that rumbling and made efforts to flee, but God's own Will kept me rooted there in place as tears streamed from my eyes. Where they touched the cracking marble, grass sprouted, grew, browned, and blew into the wind. The crumbling of rock beneath me gave way to a fissure from whose depths did grow a tree the likes of which mortal eyes were not meant to glimpse, and which I knew I should fear not because this was not a creation of the Iblis, but a beautiful manifestation of God's presence.

The tree continued to grow upwards, twisting its trunk like a grapevine towards that perfect sky, new shoots protruding from its bark as it grew with an impossibly dream-like quickness to engulf the entirety of the sky above me with leaves of the most beautiful green. Of a sudden, the tree ceased its growth, and there I stood, staring at its magnificence. This was the perfect tree, grown within the mine of God and presented before me as a gift of His love. He was showing me the beauty of His wondrous plans for this Earth, of what new growth there was here for us, His servants. There I stood, delighting in His creation, when I saw some new activity there at shoulder level on the trunk of that tree. New branches began poking through the enormous base, wriggling like worms poking through old meat, until I noticed that these were not normal branches, but fingers!

The fingers poked their way through the thick wood of the tree until I could see them as entire hands, which grasped the edges of bark and peeled them back. The wood of the tree groaned as those two powerful hands slowly pushed open a door in the trunk, bits of dirt and small pieces of tree falling to the ground at my feet but somehow avoiding my pure white dress. I was no longer afraid, confident that His hand would protect me from anything the tree could produce, confident too that this tree was indeed a source of His love and that He was going to bring forth something truly magnificent. And so, instilled with His divine confidence and my own faith, I waited until the portal into the root of the Earth finally opened.

Looking into that pit, I'd expected to see a man but all therein was deep blackness of space with hundreds of thousands of pin-prick stars shining through. There, too, I saw the swirling of countless nebulae, each one in perfect harmony with its siblings in a cosmic dance, leaving me unable to move or speak lest I shatter the perfection. I had no choice, however, in turning from the cosmos because a man coughed once, loudly, behind me!

He was about my height, slightly taller than a meter and a half, with a green turban with white and gold accents woven into the cloth wound neatly around his graying head. His wrinkled features made him appear ancient, although he did not stoop or hunch. His long, flowing beard was quite neat despite the length, and a green robe peaked out from underneath it, again with gold and white thread sewn from the shoulders down through the waist and all the way to the hem near his sandaled feet. Nothing about him spoke of wealth, yet nothing about him spoke of poverty. This was a supreme example, one of the angels, I thought.

"Quiet, girl!" He spoke in a powerful voice that didn't have the wrinkled edge I'd assumed of him or any of the normal characteristics of age that he must possess. "I'll take your prejudices into consideration should I ever choose to speak to you directly again. Walk with me for now, as this may be your last respite for quite some time."

With that, he took my hand and led me up the remaining steps and through the grass under the shade of the eternal green sky of leaves.

"I remember my last visit to your realm in the flesh," he spoke to me as we strolled. "I helped one of your 'prophets' understand the complexity of the great web that makes up the cause and effect relationships of the universe. As my metaphors were lost on him, so too were my actions, and ultimately I had to explain even the most basic of events to him in no uncertain terms."

It was then that I knew him to be Al-Khidr, and I immediately threw myself to the ground, averting my eyes.

"Get up, child! You're embarrassing me. And besides, although I told you that we do indeed have some time to enjoy in this garden, your matters are quite urgent. Furthermore, groveling is a thing of the weak, of the unworthy, or of the foolish, and you Layla, daughter of Bashir, are none of these."

I rose then to meet his gaze, strengthened by his words and now eager to hear more of his designs.

"It was not by chance that you were brought to this land so far from the cradle, daughter of Bashir. Nor is your father's research of some small import. Indeed, he has need of you beyond the mortal realm--as do all who dwell upon your planet, although they know it not." He grasped both my hands into his own, drawing me close enough to smell that his was the breath of the grave. "The one true God has seen fit to make you an instrument of His Will, and it is my job to ensure that you are prepared to do exactly what must be done to accomplish that Will. This will be your last day in this existence, so enjoy each one of its beauties with knowledge in your heart that your actions have each been blessed by Him."

As he spoke, the leaves began rotting on the tree and falling to the ground, and each leaf that touched the ground spawned worms to dig at the grass and burrow into the Earth. From each hole in the Earth came an insect, the likes of which frightened me to no end, for some of them had the faces of goats and others the faces of people and children, but all of them crawled towards me and bit at the hem of my pure white dress. Even as they began to overwhelm me, Al Khidr spoke:

"Never forget on your way, the journey that I myself took upon my last visit." He was so calm as the insects crawled up my torso, across my exposed arms, and through my hair, "Forget not what I did to the child."

With that, all vision faded from me as the insects bit at my eyes and entered my mouth. Their tiny mouths ripped small bits of meat from me as I stood there, the world becoming a mass of pain and noise, a deafening noise that squealed without ceasing.

***

I sat upright as my alarm clock squealed without ceasing, and I let it continue its noise as I panted for breath, sweat soaking through my night dress. The pain I had experienced in the dream was fading into memory as I turned to look at the red digits on the clock that were blinking repeatedly. 06:00 it read, and I slammed my hand down a little harder than usual against its top. I was alive, thanks be to God, and so I said a prayer to Him asking to remember the dream, thanking Him for His favor, and asking for wisdom on that first day of school.

Throwing my feet over the side of the bed, I noticed that my pillow was soaked with sweat which meant my hair would need brushing. I hurried into my bathroom to wash and get ready to leave the house in one and a half hours. My class schedule had come in the mail some two weeks previous. I had already committed it to memory, so great was my anticipation for this day, and I took the time alone in the shower to recall it:

Algebra 7:50 - 8:40
History 8:48 - 9:38
English 9:46 - 10:41
Art 10:49 - 11:39
Physical Education 11:47 - 12:37
Tutorials 12:37 - 1:07
Lunch 1:07 - 1:37
Economics 1:42 - 2:32
Chemistry 2:40 - 3:30

The first bell was to ring at 7:40, which meant that I only had one hour to get dressed and ready, so I washed quickly and dried quickly as well. I made sure to put on the lavender lotion, as I did every day, which was a favorite of my mother's, and dressed in my new blue jeans with the floral print blouse and matching hijab I'd set out the night before. My school back home was co-ed but had very strict dress codes, which suited me well since I had little head for fashion and preferred a more functional approach. It had taken me a full two hours the night previous to decide upon an outfit that would be suitably modest, comfortable, cute, and not too off-putting to my classmates at this new American school.

I sat brushing my hair and thought about the dream I had just experienced, how vivid it was, how real. I was convinced that its message was important, but I couldn't really comprehend whether there was meaning in the symbols I'd seen or whether I should focus my memory on the words Al-Khidr spoke to me as we walked before things turned horrible. I finished my hair, donned my hijab, and went to the kitchen for breakfast.

"There she is!" My father exclaimed. "Good morning, my flower! Are you finally ready for school?" He emphasized the word 'finally' as though I had taken hours to dress, when really it had only been one hour and here I was with twenty minutes to breakfast.

"Good morning, dad." I kissed his hairy cheek but I couldn't shake what Al-Khidr had mentioned. "What are you researching here again?"

He stopped pouring his coffee and looked up at me, confused because I had never mentioned his job, studies, or research before that moment, I realize now. He turned to regard me for what felt like the first time.

"It has to do with the electromagnetic spectrum," he said, rather unsure as he went back to his coffee. "And carrier waves. Why the sudden interest in my work, love?"

"I don't know," I replied, pouring my cereal. "I just thought maybe it was pretty important to you and I've never asked you about it at all." Through mouthfuls I added, "Besides, I love you, Dad. And I'm really happy we're here together."

"You want money already?" he said as he reached mockingly for his wallet. "It's the first day of your sophomore year, and here you are, already robbing me!" We both laughed as we finished up our breakfast, me with my cereal, him with his cell phone, news and coffee. "Well, we'd better get you off to school."

The school was only some three kilometers from our house, and he drove me right up to the front steps, where I leaned over across the gear shift and gave him another kiss on the cheek.

"Have a good day, Layla. I'll see you after school!" I waved before turning nervously towards the steps.

There were plenty of students on the front lawn and in the entryway as I walked up the steps. Some were in pairs chatting about this or that, others were in big groups laughing, some boys were making lewd gestures in a circle and there was even a group of kids kicking a football off by some trees. Nobody said a word to me as I entered the school, but that was okay with me since I was worried that if someone spoke to me the butterflies in my belly would fly from my mouth. There was a little table set up in the main entryway with maps and schedules and a round, middle-aged lady in a purple dress sitting behind it. A sign behind her head read "Welcome New Students."

"Hi there, sugar." She sounded like the squirrel from SpongeBob. "You must be new here. Name?"

"Layla Bashir"

"Bash-ear, Bash-ear," she muttered as she looked through a stack of papers. When she turned back to me she spoke more slowly, as though English were as foreign to me as Arabic undoubtedly was to her. "Here you are! This is a little map for you to show you where to go." She was highlighting specific rooms on the map. "The yell-oh rooms are yours. For PE, you just go down to the changing room downstairs in the gym first. OK?"

"Thanks," I said, taking the map and schedule.

I turned away from the woman--Barbara, her name tag said. I oriented myself to the small map and checked for my Algebra class.

Once I had the map figured out, I walked directly towards the classroom--which was on the first floor, thankfully. I was quite certain I would have tripped if I'd tried any more stairs at that point, with my heart pounding behind my ribs. The bell had not rung yet and the class was nearly empty.

"Take any seat you like," said a handsome young man with black hair, bushy eyebrows, a blue polo shirt and khaki pants from behind a desk piled high with text books. He must have been the professor. "We'll call roll after the bell."

I took a seat near the window and placed my bag on the floor beside my desk. I unzipped the black backpack and pulled out a notebook and pencil, then closed my backpack and sat attentively as the bell rang loudly from the hall. More students took seats throughout the room, leaving ample space around me.

"Come on, come on. Quickly now," the teacher said as he turned around to write his name on the board. "Take your seats quickly so we can get started."

Finally, a boy slumped down next to me. He had scruffy brown hair, freckles, and a pair of glasses. He dropped his bag unceremoniously on the ground near me and looked around. I noticed his clothes were clean but definitely not new, perhaps secondhand, with corduroy pants, Converse shoes, and a grey t-shirt with some image on the front that was obscured by the desk.

"Hey," he directed to me. His breath was fresh with mint as though he had only recently brushed before class. "Nice scarf. What's your name?"

As I opened my mouth to reply, the professor began calling roll. I shut my mouth and nodded my head towards the teacher. The boy and I shifted our gaze to him.

"As I call your name, raise your hand and say 'here'," he began. "Jonathan Atbury?" There was a brief pause, a student said "here", and he continued down the list until he got to my name. "Layla Bashir?"

"Here," I said.

The teacher, 'Mr. Statler' from the whiteboard, looked up. "You're Doctor Bashir's daughter, aren't you?"

I could feel myself blushing, but nodded anyway.

"Glad to have you in class. Maybe you'll be teaching me a thing or two," he chuckled and continued with his list until he called out, "Zachary Nolan?" The boy sitting next to me raised his hand. "I'm now going to pass out textbooks. You'll notice I've placed the curriculum and class schedule in the front of each book. Now these books have to last all year, so make sure to cover them tonight at home to make them last! I doubt there is any money in the budget for new books, so just be good to them, okay?"

Zachary nudged me and gave me a small folded paper with the word "Zack" written next to a ten-digit number. I placed it in my Algebra book and blushed even deeper while reading over my curriculum and trying to listen to the teacher. Mr. Statler went into great detail about what we'd be covering and why it was important, although nobody could understand the use of algebra (even me), but there we sat until the bell rang and we were excused for the ten minutes until our next class.

As I was gathering up my things, Zack said, "Layla huh? That's a cool name. What's your next class?"

"History, room 214."

"Right on. My class is upstairs too… Remedial English. I'll walk with you."

We put our backpacks on and started walking towards the stairwell. I got some weird looks from a group of beautiful girls who were chatting amongst themselves and snickering, but I didn't really mind. An American boy was walking me to class! I'd have to tell my friends back home about this, although I'd make sure to exaggerate his appearance. We made our way through the crowded halls and up the staircase towards our destinations.

"So is your dad some kind of, uh, mathematician or something?"

"Physicist."

"Whoa, he must be pretty famous for Statler to mention it! Listen, why don't you call me sometime, and we can hang out?"

"Sure," I said. "This is my class."

"OK. Adios!"

The next four periods were uneventful. More of the same thing, just introductions and getting books, curricula, schedules and the like. Nobody else talked with me, though. Nobody even said hello other than the teachers. I was definitely lonely and the day seemed to drag on, even through a solitary lunch. I hoped I would bump into Zack again so at the very least I'd have someone to sit with, but no, I sat alone at a table near the large window overlooking the track I'd been on a couple hours earlier.   In fact, the rest of the day was entirely uneventful--until last period, that is, when Zack showed up in the chemistry lab. He walked right over to my workspace, which was definitely solitary up until that moment, and set his bags down.

"How's it going?" he asked. "Got a partner yet?"

"No."

"Sweet. Do you mind? Chemistry is my shit!"

I had heard this used before in a positive manner but it was still odd to me to use a vulgar word in such a way, so I wrinkled my nose a bit but smiled anyway, ecstatic to have someone friendly around me again. The class went exactly like those before it, so Zack and I chatted quietly about video games we'd played and bands we liked. We watched a safety video for the final quarter hour of class. When the bell rang, I was feeling very good but also eager to get home and start on the history report that was due in two weeks. History was not easy for me and so I made every effort to study my hardest for it, especially since it was American history, which I knew next to nothing about.

Zack walked beside me out of the school, our backpacks full of text books, and down the steps to the sidewalk that went to my house. He asked me which direction I was heading and when I pointed towards my house he said he was going the opposite way and that we'd see each other tomorrow. I agreed and waved goodbye as I walked the three kilometers home, feeling oddly exhausted and energized after such a long day at school, but definitely hungry and ready to put down my now full backpack.

As I approached my house, I couldn't shake the feeling that something was wrong, like there was something urgent going on nearby that I should avoid. I slowed my pace and looked around, but there was my dad's car parked just so in the driveway, the chain link fence was closed and there was nothing odd about our small yard. When I approached the front door, however, I noticed it was slightly ajar and I heard a thumping coming from inside. I set my bag down and prayed for God to give me courage and make me silent as I pushed the door open enough to go inside and investigate.

The thumping continued, but now I could hear a gurgling also, all coming from the direction of the office which was just around the corner from the kitchen. I don't know how or why, but as I crept through the kitchen, I took the large knife from the block on the counter and held it down by my side, point backwards and edge facing the floor as I moved with all the commotion of a shadow towards the sound from around the corner. God is merciful, God is great, I chanted in my head as I crouched before the double doors to the office, doors that were pushed open onto a scene that I couldn't quite comprehend at first.

A very large back and extremely large set of shoulders covered in a grey jacket was crouched over something--or someone, as I noticed two feet sticking out from underneath the shape. The shoes were the same brown leather loafers that I'd seen every day for the entirety of my existence, and they were drumming against the ground with a thumping noise as that hulking form crouched over what I knew was my father. It only took an instant for me to recognize that my father was being killed there in our house, that this inhumanly huge shape was strangling his life from his lungs and that those gurgling sounds were the last that I'd hear from my father.

I closed the distance from the door to the brute quickly, all the while reciting the name of God in my mind and pleading with him to lend me His strength. I lifted the knife steadily from my side until my fist was near my temple, knife tip pointing to the meat just under the ribs on the side, the place where the kidneys are, and brought it down quickly. I retracted my hand and repeated the motion, again towards the same spot, now towards the other side and then I threw myself onto that back. With the first stab, the shape jerked rigid and rolled back onto its heels, the second and third had it bringing its arms backwards to swat me off while it twisted to face me. I was too quick and succeeded in keeping my face to his back until I was able to throw my legs around the back and my left arm around its neck.

"Allahu Akbar!" I yelled as I plunged the knife down from the base of his neck and into his body, again and again. I yelled even as the body toppled back and to the side with me still clinging, still stabbing at the neck. Blood was everywhere: on my arms, my fist, my face. Hot and red it was coming out of the body, being pumped from the sides and onto my thighs that still gripped the corpse. I rolled out from under the body and dropped the knife to the floor, blood collecting around it on the fine rug of my father's office. I came around to my father, cradling his head in my lap as tears poured from my eyes, knowing full well that he was no more and praying out loud for God to show his divine mercy on him.

God's Might left me then, as I slumped there with my father's body on my lap, crying, with blood sticking my hands to the sides of his head, and I lay my own head down on his, forehead to forehead. Minutes or hours later, I looked up from his face to his chest, where his hands were still clutching something even now, even after the life had left him. I sat up and gently prised the fingers away from a metal box no larger than my father's Samsung, which I took into my hands and examined. It was not heavy, but seemed definitely durable, the kind into which you'd place something for travel if you knew that the baggage handlers would not necessarily be gentle. I opened the little hinge and inside there was a small black gem which gave me the vague impression of a crystal, but did not gleam whatsoever. Curious, I held it up to the light that was streaming in through a window near the assailant's corpse.

It was only then that I noticed the face of my father's murderer.

3

Zeke's house was so cluttered with books and stacks of papers that I was instantly reminded of the crazy dude in every movie, the conspiracy theorist who puts photographs and newspaper clippings up on the walls and, in a maddening attempt to visualize the paranoid connections he's somehow dreamt up, pins bits of red string from one photograph to another regardless of any obstructions something as simple as household logistics might pose.

His newspapers weren't stacked and dusty like I'd originally thought. These were new, but appeared to be from every corner of the globe. Some had awkward, cramped little boxes of Chinese characters, others the flowing script of the Arabs, and some had the near-Tolkeinian shape of Thai script. It was hard not to notice, even as quickly as we were moving, the theme of the books that were scattered throughout as well.

Bibles, Qur'ans, holy books of every denomination, from the most well-established to the most cultish, were open on the arms of chairs, their spines facing the ceiling, or piled on couch cushions. He walked directly through the maze, picked up a wide tome bound in red leather with what looked like gold metal lining the edges and a chain wrapped all around it, and stuffed it into his satchel without so much as a glance in my direction.

The snapping of trees and rumbling of earth were growing louder as we opened the back door of his house and headed to the ancient-looking garage. He threw the barn-style doors open, revealing a late model Toyota truck, some sawhorses, various woodworking instruments and yard tools. He grabbed a machete and threw it to me before going to the driver's side of the truck. We both hopped into the cab, and before the doors were shut he had it running. Despite the impending doom we both felt, Zeke pulled out slow and smooth, veering off the gravel that made up his driveway onto a crudely formed dirt road that maps would not even label as 'unimproved'.

"Can't take the main roads. No telling how many are moving around out there," he mumbled nervously. "This road'll work for a while. Meets up with a firebreak few miles in. Maybe long enough to outrun him, buy us some time. Yeah."

I only half-listened while watching the woods behind his house get smaller in the side-view mirror, a large cloud of dust and forest debris moving in the direction from which we'd come. It was only then that I started to feel the exhaustion of what I'd just been through: the frantic dash through the woods, my companions likely crushed underneath logs; a visit to a madman's sanctuary, dusty tomes with hand-drawn demons, geometric shapes in red, pentagrams, crosses, the crescent and the star...

***

Ozzy, my cat, kept pace with me as we ran away from the chaos that had become of our Seattle suburb. We'd purchased him after I came back from a temporary duty in Germany some three years previous, and he was a great mouser. Not the most graceful cat, but a killing machine. My pack was light and my boots were long since broken in, so it seemed like we were making incredible speed even in the dark of night. A car would have been much quicker, but I'd seen too many incidents of mass chaos where everyone within city limits attempts to flee from one tragedy or another simultaneously. No, this was the perfect time for a jog in the woods.

I had no compulsion for heroism while escaping with my life, no thought to run through the streets shouting for people to wake up and evacuate. This wasn't like being in line at a corner store when some thug tries to hold the place up. You don't just disarm some force large enough to conquer Seattle in a matter of hours and spread in a 30-mile radius. Nor was it a time for speculation, but old habits die hard and I found myself contemplating how it was that the Chinese were able to bring enough of a ground presence to push like they were into the areas outside the city. This artillery barrage had to come from somewhere.

Parked ahead, visible from the woods lining the road, was an old Honda motorcycle. I altered my path to get a closer look and see if I could use it in my flight. Ozzy followed along at my heels, still keeping pace despite his size. I got close enough to confirm my suspicions that this was just the model for me, and flipped my backpack off a shoulder and onto my belly like a kangaroo. I unzipped the outside pocket and pulled from it a small pocket knife, zipped the pocket, and flipped the backpack back over my shoulder by the time I made it to the bike. I unfolded the thin blade, stabbed it into the ignition and turned it until the small lights on the late '80s display panel turned on and light blasted from the front of the bike.

"Good luck, cat," I said, swinging my leg over the saddle. "I'm sure you've got at least four lives left."

Ozzy looked up at me, his eyes pleading and deploring at once, and then he ran off into the darkness as I turned the engine over and pulled away from the curb.

***

A sharp bump brought me back to the Toyota with a feeling of regret and loss, along with two stinging thighs, an aching back, and two burning feet. I must have made some kind of pained face along with the long groan, because Zeke pointed to a bottle of pills in the cup holder. I shook out two and swallowed them down with a drink from a bottle of water that was rolling around near my feet as we drove along down that same dirt road. I must have been out for a while though, since the thick forest had thinned out enough to offer great visibility of the surrounding area. The road had taken us into an agricultural area as we passed between rows of hops hanging down from trellises.

"Did you get a good look at them?" Zeke asked without looking at me.

"Nope," I breathed. "Saw 'em take out my neighborhood that first night and I've been running ever since."

"Shit. This ain't the Chinese, boy. Not the Koreans, neither. How'd they get here so quick, huh? And spread so fast?"

"Sleeper agents," I responded immediately, as this was the only rational explanation I'd come up with in the few weeks following the invasion. "Seattle gets thousands of immigrants per month, either with student visas, work visas, or illegally in shipping containers. Hundreds of thousands, all groomed to strike at the signal of their handlers here stateside. Their signal was a cell phone outage, and they knew to get into position at the various Army Reserve units and Naval units. Base security is a joke at those places, and the only resistance they'd face would be a cursory force. I mean, look at when they struck: midnight on a pay day. Any personnel who could be called up would be too drunk to do anything, and the gate guards or fireguards or whatever would be too disgruntled and distracted to offer any resistance--not against thousands of bodies. Shit, they'd be lucky to pop off a couple shots, let alone get a phone call out. There have to be a few new soldiers on Lewis from overseas too, what with the MAVNI program giving citizenship to them just for signing up. They'd have access to everything: tanks, helicopters, you name it. Hell, we trained them, for fuck's sake."

"Sounds like a decent theory, except for one thing."

"Oh, yeah? What's that?"

"The fucking DRAGON in the rear-view."

4

In the name of God, the most merciful, the beneficent, supreme ruler of all that is good and judge of those foul things at the fringe of our existence, the horrors that were unleashed upon my mind in that very moment of realization, as my eyes sent precious electricity to my brain which at first could not interpret the signals correctly, still haunt me despite those initial moments being tame compared to the atrocities I have since faced in the Name of God's Divine Justice. Indeed, even in comparison to that first illuminating visit from Al-Khidr, where terror was the punctuation to an otherwise divine experience, seeing in the flesh one of Iblis' servants--corpse though it now was--was enough to drive all thought from my mind until I too lay on the floor, unconscious. As now that original visage is beautiful in comparison to the monstrosities that God has deemed enemy, in those illuminating moments it obliterated all other thoughts from my mind.

The shape of that djinn was almost entirely that of a human being, as God had at one time favored all of His creations to include such devils, with the exception of the face. My father, God rest his soul, lay splayed across the rug, his face still tight at the eyes and lips blue from suffocation but otherwise recognizable. His face was not much changed from when it contorted in rage the time when I was but a child and spilled ink all over the tie with the chevron pattern. The one that was a gift from Mother, God rest her soul. The djinn, on the other hand, held no such expression. Indeed, there was no expression at all.

When the body rolled away from my father, God rest his soul, my attention was entirely on whether or not life remained within the poor doctor. When I finally beheld that face, its hypnotism must have faded, although I was only slightly less entranced. The black hair on top of its head hung down across what was meant to be a forehead and sideburns encircled the place that should have contained a nose and mouth. Indeed, the most horrifying, most mesmerizing aspect was that in place of normal human features, there was nothing but the vastness of deep space.

The swirling nebulae and stars were all moving far more noticeably than when I observed the sky on clear nights back home with my eyes unaided. It was as though the whole of the universe was involved in some sort of intricate dance, like the movements of a bumblebee as it communicates the location of a particularly rich pollen source to its mates. I felt my body move of its own volition towards that face, against the wishes of the remaining part of my consciousness, which seemed tiny and muted against the force of the cosmos merely a meter from me. As I stared into the depths of space, tiny mysteries were beginning to take root in my mind, like the earliest sprouts from a seed in fertile earth. Time, energy, sacred geometry--God would be revealed therein, and each of the million stars spoke directly to my mind, promising epiphanies as numerous as grains of sand.

Even as I strained against my body's involuntary momentum, the lights began to lose their luster, the dust slowed its swirling, and the comets winked out. Indeed, the great blackness that composed the backdrop for the interstellar dance began to fade into opacity, revealing an exact cross section of the contents of a human skull. It was as though a person's face was crudely hacked away from the rest of the head, perhaps the result of an industrial machine accident or being mauled by a bear, and rather than scabbing over in the normal way that a cut to the leg or hand would, a film developed in which a galaxy was contained. When the light of the galaxy faded, the only thing left was unhealed gore and a transparent sack of some otherworldly mucus.

With that hypnotic galactic mucus sack draining in front of my eyes, my bodily control was returned to me and with it, the scream that I had been issuing all along immediately exploded from my mouth. I clamped my hands over my lips to stifle it, but God's truth, I could not contain the noise that I made for what seemed like hours. So much oxygen had escaped my mouth as I knelt there amongst the dead that my head began swimming and I started seeing stars, thanks be to God not the kind that come from the Faceless Ones, but rather the stars that come as one loses consciousness and collapses on the corpse of their father.

***

Al-Khidr was waiting for me the moment my eyes opened in the chemistry lab at my new American school, his green robes and wizened features comforting me after such an ordeal as I'd never dreamed possible. Why I appeared there, at a school I barely knew in a country in which I was an alien I'll never know, but it did provide some odd sense of relief to be amongst the blackboards, computers, vials and burners of a place of learning.

I was wearing black now, a hijab, long-sleeved blouse and pants, rather than the white dress I'd worn previously, and in my hands was the same small metal box I'd recovered from father, God rest his soul. I brought the small metal box up near my face and started to lift the lid when Al-Khidir's hands clamped against my own, preventing me from exposing the contents.

"Never again, Layla," he hissed, "should you lift that lid, though it will remain with you until the end of your days. Never again should your atmosphere touch that THING whether dreaming or waking. Maintain it you must, but never again should that box be opened."

I nodded and lowered the box.

"The Faceless One is but a pawn in the armies of the night. His abilities, as you may have ascertained, are based on the crudest of the senses and he has no sway over the sixth or seventh, nor the ninth. You know him vulnerable and now should fear him not. Your task has begun, however, and I fear that I may only come to you once more before the final Judgment, although perhaps in another form or realm. So now I must give you one last weapon before the curtain falls."

With that, he took the index finger of his right hand and placed it on the crown of my skull. He drew a line down my forehead, across my nose, lips and chin, all the way down my neck to my trachea just above my collar bone. I felt an intense heat all along that line, and he raised both hands to either side of my face, cleaving my skull on that mystic seam through skin, bone, brain and tongue until my face was open like the spine of a book. I could indeed see behind me while my face was opened like this, giving me a sense of nausea, although there was no pain as Al-Khidr parted my skull.

I then felt him place something hot into the innermost part of my brain, something that--even turned as my eyes were--emitted a light bright enough to leave lines in my vision after he snapped my face shut. As the lines began to fade, however I noticed a difference in my own vision immediately, in that place, the realm of the dreamer. I cannot describe the subtle change I noticed but suffice it to say that I now perceived even the dream landscape with a new vision.

"This is all that remains of my gifts," he said as his form began to fade. "It will not be enough on its own, but you may stand some small chance in the face of the Nameless ones now. Until next we meet." As he faded, so too did the walls, desks and various implements of science from my American chemistry lab, until I realized that my eyes were slowly opening to the original scene of carnage that I left behind.

***

Only when the walls fully coalesced around me and I could see the Faceless One and my father, God rest his soul, both slumped there on the floor did I realize that in addition to the grisly sight of two bodies, their various fluids outside of them for the first time, there was also a horrible odor. I stood up, gagging, and stumbled out of the room, hands glued to the small box between them as I stepped over the Faceless One and back into the kitchen. I must have been out for a few hours because the light that had come in through the kitchen windows was now turning into sunset, leaving me with an impending sense of dread for the coming night. I did not want to fathom the countless horrors that awaited me since the brazen attack of one of their number upon my house in daylight. What terrors could they unleash in their natural climate?

I caught my reflection in the stainless steel toaster that sat on top of the counter near the refrigerator and was appalled by the bloody young woman I saw quivering there. At that moment, there was nothing more important in the world than cleansing myself of the terrible carnage that I had wrought that afternoon. I made my way through the house and into my bedroom, where I placed the box on my night stand and peeled the blood-crusted clothes from my head and body before turning on the faucet and stepping into the shower.

As the water rushed over my matted hair and crusted hands, it came away the color of rust, and I scrubbed with soap until there were no more impurities to that life-giving substance. While I scrubbed at the evidence of my encounter with a creature of the night, my brain could not relax in the way that my skin did. It finally dawned on me that I was entirely alone in the world, without even a single friend, in a foreign country, with people who considered me a terrorist, a 16-year-old Osama bin Laden, so I prayed to God to help me.

I said His names aloud as the water purified me. "Al Rahman, Al Raheem, Al Maleek, Al Qudoos, Al Salaam, Al Mumeen…." With each subsequent name of the hundred, my mind became clearer. Indeed, God above answered my prayers as He had never done before. A supreme and infinite clarity filled me to the brim as I turned the knobs of the faucet to the right and dried myself. After toweling dry, I pulled my black sports hijab from the top shelf of my dresser, along with matching sports underwear, then went to my closet to get the long-sleeved shirt and loose black pants from where they hung.

I pulled out two similar uniforms, laid them on the bed next to the metal box, and ran outside to fetch the backpack I'd abandoned when I came upon that terrible scene what seemed a lifetime ago. Then I went to my father's room and into his closet. After emptying my pack of the now useless texts and curricula, I pulled my passport and an envelope of money from the box underneath the slacks which hung neatly from a rod. Moving the box aside revealed a small door leading to the crawl space below our house, from which I pulled another much smaller box. Inside was the set of matching knives my grandfather had given my father, God rest their souls, when he'd graduated from University.

The blades were as long as my forearm, curved with plain hilts, the handles covered in soft black leather matching the sheathes in which they stayed. Had I unsheathed them, they would have shown with the distinct glow of pure silver. I took them, leaving the box behind, and pushed them, my passport, and our life savings into the bottom of my backpack before returning to my room where I proceeded to fill my pack with the clothes and the metal box.

Confident that I had enough clothes to accomplish God's plan, I went to the kitchen to do the same for food. I made sure to eat while I put the nonperishable food stuffs into the rapidly filling backpack, awareness that I may not have a similar opportunity to eat for a long time yet settled over me like armor against the coming onslaught. Once I was certain I had enough food to last for about a week with proper rationing, I set my pack to my shoulders and pulled the cigarette lighter from the junk drawer by the dishwasher as I went to the garage for the can of gasoline.

5

I glanced at the side mirror to discover that Zeke wasn't lying. There, with its head and shoulders sticking up above the wood-line, was a huge fucking monster crashing through the forest directly behind us. We had about a mile on the creature, although judging by the size of those massive shoulders, it looked like it would close the distance even quicker once it cleared what remained of the woods. The first thing I noticed about the beast was the enormous shoulders; each looked to be the size of a house all in grey with bristles sticking up that must have been as thick as telephone poles to be seen at this distance. The head was roughly the size of two school buses sitting side-by-side, with a wide forehead that pulled back like I would imagine on a Cro-Magnon, an inbred human or perhaps a gorilla. The brow ridge had two enormous tufts that spilled past the curve of the face and into the distance behind it, and farther down, the cheeks were very high and round, leading to a remarkably human-like nose.

The majority of the damned thing's face was mouth, a mouth that was turned up at the corners contorted into a madcap grin, like that of a rapist who has beaten his target into submission and is near his final glory. Disgustingly, it had the flat and broad yellow teeth of a human smoker, although there were far too many crowded together and it seemed like there was another row behind the first. The mouth was so large that it creased the grey skin at the corners of the eyes…

I stuck my head completely out of the passenger-side window, not caring that the bumpy ride smashed me against the door frame, needing a closer look. Debris was flying in every direction as the dark grey shape barreled through trees and terrain alike without pause. I had to get a good look at those eyes. They reminded me of something, somewhere, that I couldn't quite discern from merely turning in my seat. I heard noises coming from the driver's side but there was something wrong with him, like he was talking with cotton in his mouth, so I ignored him entirely to focus on the two swimming pools in the middle of that disgusting face.

They were enormous, a blue so deep I could not imagine any other color, so familiar my mind focused on them entirely like trying to remember an old song. There were other colors there, too: yellow, white, purple and green, all moving. The longer I looked, the more familiar it all felt, images of the Hubble Telescope sprang to mind and suddenly the skin around my eyes, my eyebrows and upper cheeks started to burn as I heard laughter from far off. My eyes grew hotter and hotter until something cracked at the back of my skull.

***

I woke up face down on somebody's lawn. I was awoken by the heat on the back of my head and arms, which gave me the impression that it must be mid-afternoon. The motorcycle was a few yards to my right in the middle of the sidewalk with dirt and chunks of grass sticking out of the front tire. I pushed myself up and looked around me as I moved to a sitting position to get my bearings. I had ridden the stolen Honda all night--that much I remembered--then I hit a pothole as the sun started to rise and woke up here.

With the mystery solved, I rose to my feet and did a quick equipment check, dug around in my pack and grabbed my cell phone. It took a moment to turn on, and when it finally did, there was absolutely no signal. I tried to force a call anyway, only to get a message about no signal and contact my provider. Instead of contacting AT&T, I turned the thing off, stuffed it in my backpack, and took out a protein bar while

I started walking south.

It took me a while to notice, but there were no people at all in this neighborhood, although there was evidence of their recent evacuation. Doors open wide, skid marks in the road, etc. I quickened my pace. With an eerie sense of dread, I made for the woods when I heard voices coming from up ahead in the distance.

***

"Snap the fuck out of it!" Zeke was screaming as we barreled down the road. "Wake the fuck up, man! I'm gonna need you goddamn it!"

I couldn't stop giggling, but moaned as I felt an ache in the back of my head.

"Shit, man, that's it." He was slapping me in the face. "Snap out of it."

My face was on fire as the giggling gave way to coughing and I struggled to open my eyes. I was wet and I could only open my eyes to slits, but what I saw made me gag. My fingers were contorted on my lap into claws and there were bits of skin and blood dripping from each one. I relaxed them and reached for my head as I flipped down the vanity visor to take a look at my face. Blood was oozing from my eyebrows and cheeks as I realized that I had made an insane attempt to dig out my eyes at some point during our ride.

"Wha..." I mumbled, wiping my brow with my sleeve. I found some napkins in the glove box and wet them with the remaining water from the bottle I'd used earlier, cleaning the disgusting gashes I'd made.

"You started laughing like a madman," Zeke explained, jerking on the wheel to avoid a rock. "Then you stuck your head out the window like you wanted to jump, scratching at your face the whole time. I threw my tire iron at you and hauled your ass back in here. You're welcome."

"Thanks."

We clattered down the road for some time longer, me nursing multiple wounds, him glancing in the rear view occasionally--without the same reaction that I had.

"How is it that you keep looking at that thing without turning into some kind of lunatic?" But I didn't get an answer because up ahead, two objects appeared in the air growing larger by the second. It only took a few seconds for me to recognize the familiar shapes of those two guardian angels as they sped towards us, and I was comforted to know that in a matter of seconds the nightmare creature that had been pursuing me for weeks would suddenly become well acquainted with two 30mm cannons and a metric shit ton of 500-lb bombs.

6

In the name of God, the merciful and just, when my home caught flame as the sun set in the west, more than just a house and much more than what remained of my family was taken away from the earth. My father, God rest his soul, was the last person on the planet related to me by blood after the rest were destroyed in the bloody war my country experienced when I was too young to realize that there was a world outside the chaos of smoke, fire, blood and noise. With the events of the day, I had plunged my own world back into that maddening version of reality from which we fled. Knowledge that my actions were done in the Name of God was little solace.

Indeed, as I felt the heat rising from my father's corpse and quietly exited the house, I could feel the last traces of hope and love come out of the corners of my eyes, carried by tears that would not stop even as I ran through the wilderness. The blaze was enormous enough to cause a cloud of smoke to cover the horizon, and a small part of me worried that other houses may have joined with the dancing flames, but I didn't look back over my shoulder to see the yellow and red breaking the solitude of black that had become of the sky.

A guilt gnawed at my heart then, alone amongst the shrubs and sparse grass of the endless pastures and wild lands, a guilt that stemmed from my own selfish desires being gone to me. Here I was free to study in the open, to walk in a park with a boy. I had the opportunity to wear western clothes, not the bulky sack I had back home, with nobody to enforce God's law but my own conscience. In this land, nobody would want to kidnap me and sell me. Here I would have been able to do gymnastics for the high school team and compete in front of males and females. Now, though, I was back where I started, and the guilt of that knowledge pushed hot liquid from my eyes which would not even dry with the warm wind buffeting my face as I ran through the growing darkness.

My legs began to remind me of the distance I'd run even before my eyes noticed the growing light from the east, and indeed they gave out, depositing my body at the base of a bush whose name I did not know. I dragged myself with my arms underneath the bush, feeling moans force their way past my lips as I curled around its base and sobbed myself to sleep.

I heard a sloppy mouth chewing some distance nearby, but my sore eyes didn't want to open after the tragedy they had witnessed. Pushing away from the bush and into the open, I slowly pushed up into a sitting position and forced my eyes open to see where exactly my frantic flight left me. A cow munched grass a few meters away, paying me no mind while I stretched the stiffness out of my neck and back. Legs shaking, I stood to get a little more blood to my two sore feet but quickly decided that sitting was better after my midnight trail run. As I rubbed my thighs, I noticed how desperately thirsty I was so I dumped my backpack out on the ground beside me searching for a bottle of water and a little something to eat.

Food, clothes, water bottles and knives were all there, but the thing that caught my attention was that metal box, the one that seemed a catalyst to my world's end. Even as I opened a bottle and pressed it to my lips, my eyes didn't leave that box, not even when I had drunk my fill and started on a breakfast bar did I avert those tired orbs from it.

With a brief prayer to God, I picked up the box with both hands. It was cool to the touch, which came as no surprise, but even as I slowly pried open the lid I could feel a heat spill out around me. With the top fully off and the crystal exposed, I got a chance to see it as if for the first time and was instantly repulsed by some unknown sense of dread that started at my fingers and emanated through the very core of my being. The black crystal had perplexing angles that didn't seem quite right and I felt the same impossible magnetism that I had when seeing the Faceless One what seemed years ago. I shut the lid quickly with the revelation that the two must have some connection, and shoved the box to the very bottom of my bag, burying it under my clothes, food and water. The knives I left at the top.

The sun was well on its journey west as I relieved myself behind that bush, cleaned up and hefted the pack onto my shoulders, but I got the distinct impression that I was no longer alone there amongst the sporadic grass and brush. Looking around, I saw nothing out of the ordinary, just me, the wilderness, the sky and that cow, who was no longer chewing but staring directly at me with those unsettling black eyes. Instinct told me to move slowly away, which I did, and to pull a knife from my pack, which I also did. Those two black eyes remained firmly attached to me as I moved in the same direction I'd been traveling the previous night.

I quickened my steps, looking over my shoulder occasionally, but the beast had not stirred except to move that great head in my direction as I moved farther and farther away. There was a barbed wire fence ahead, which instinct again told me to put between the two of us as sweat began to pour from my underarms and behind my hijab. The light was fading too quickly and I wasn't near enough the fence, but a look over my shoulder ensured that the creature a few hundred meters away was stationary.

Half-jogging, I moved with all haste towards the fence as the light around me changed to a brilliant pink that I knew would soon turn the deep purple of night on the open plain, scared now like the girl I once was but without so much as a thin blanket under which to hide. A check over my shoulder. The cow, some half-kilometer behind, was now shaking its head with a quickness I knew impossible, even with my limited knowledge of livestock. Foam spit was flying around its head as it convulsed openly, and I broke into a run for the remaining few hundred meters to the fence. My heart was beating against my rib cage, blood and adrenaline flowing equally upon my approach and, gifted with God's ability, I jumped over the fence onto a dirt road.

Although I cleared the fence neatly, my landing left me tumbling in the dirt just as the sky above turned dark.

Sprawling in the dirt, I looked back at the cow far beyond the fence, my breath catching in my throat. The silhouette of its horns was jerkily growing longer as a dull red mist splashed from the skull with the sudden new growth. The elongated horns made a creaking sound, audible even from this distance, slightly muted by an unnatural growl coming from the beast's throat. It arched its back upward like a stretching cat, and I could see distinct ridges pressing from the vertebra. More bellows came from its mouth, which was hanging open and now dripping a slightly viscous fluid. When the transformation was complete from cow to djinn, it stamped its feet and began a charge.

Scrambling to my feet, I gripped the handle of the knife until my knuckles went white and began running down the dirt road with every ounce of strength in my body. The sound grew louder by the second but I didn't dare turn around as I pushed my legs for all remaining speed. The name of God escaped my lips as headlights shined from up ahead. He had answered my prayers, I knew. The lights were blinding, but as the driver noticed me he dimmed them to parking and approached slowly. Just then I heard a commotion and risked a glance over my shoulder. The servant of Iblis had thrown itself through the fence and was now charging directly behind me, a tangle of hooves, froth, and now barbed wire, ready to trample me into submission.

The car stopped in the middle of the road and the driver's door opened just ahead of me, as the beast made rapid progress a mere 100 meters behind. God willed me to jump directly on the hood and continue over the cab of the truck, sliding into the bed, as I heard the driver cuss loudly and slam the door shut. We were both too late.

The impact of a ton of flesh striking the front of the truck threw me over the tailgate and into the dirt, but it pushed the engine block into the cab of the truck. Pushing myself to my feet, I scrambled for the knife which had fallen from my hand as I hit the ground. The driver moaned and cussed with his remaining breath, pinned gruesomely to the metal of his vehicle, the cow thrashing about unconcerned with its predicament. It took mere seconds for me to retrieve the knife, but then I was torn as to whether or not to return to the truck. Praying out loud gave me courage, and the Will of God pushed me to the wreckage, each step giving me courage as I brought the knife level with my shoulder held in reverse with the point toward my elbow.

The terrible creature had twisted, strange growths had developed around its head and the once small horns were longer although less symmetrical. Dark red blood was visible from the working headlamp that was somehow connected to electricity, and it was plain from the gore spewing onto the wrinkled front half of the truck that the force of impact had jammed the beast's skull between its shoulders. Despite being so obviously defeated, the head moved upon my approach, mouth gaping and bloody with the remains of a hideously enlarged tongue lolling against now jagged and distinctly pointed teeth. It made every effort to continue in its designs as I blessed it in the name of God and pressed the point of the knife into the jet black eyes until the jelly spilled over my fist. With a final shudder, the remaining life left its body and a strange sense of peace settled over me.

Gurgling from the cab made me look up to notice the poor driver still had some life left in him, so I left the knife in the eye socket of that monster and ran to his side. Through the window I grasped his hand in mine and touched his cheek with the other, tears streaming once more from my eyes as I began praying for his safe journey to God's Kingdom. He could no longer speak, but I held him in that manner, kissing his forehead and speaking softly to him until his chin dropped against his chest and his spirit departed.

7

The A-10 Warthog was designed for close air support missions against ground-based targets. It's not the Top Gun F-14 Tomcat that can pound and evade enemy aircraft. No, the A-10 fires bullets the length of your palm full to the brim with depleted uranium at a rate of about 65 per second. Warthogs were made to fly quickly towards a tank or fortified position and rip it apart from the sky without having to put friendly personnel and equipment at risk. The armor is thicker than on most ground vehicles, they travel somewhere in the neighborhood of 300mph, and they unleash Hell from an altitude of a thousand-some-odd feet in the air. And two of them were on approach to my position.

From the passenger side window, I watched the two jets approach side-by-side at a rate of speed that would have halted any conversation within the car if we weren't both already dumbfounded by the awe of modern engineering that was about to save our asses. I held a filthy rag to my face to sop up the blood while Zeke's foot stayed glued to the accelerator. We bumped between Washington hops with a sense of relief the likes of which I had not felt since the moment of my eldest son's birth.

The pounding from the dragon stopped when it realized that it wasn't the only apex predator in the area, so I risked a glance backward to watch the destruction unfold, making dead certain to avoid those hypnotic eyes. It stopped in its tracks at the edge of the field and rolled its body weight back and onto two gigantic, grey scaly haunches, like a cat ready to bat the play end of a feather toy. Even seated like that, the monster must have been the size of a high-rise apartment building with a belly armored in two rows of pale, grey plates as big as city buses.

Two Avenger cannons started spinning overhead as the planes began their approach, but the dragon's stomach tightened visibly like it was trying to force something up. Its neck and head drew back and constricted while bullets smacked the earth just ahead of it, creating a spray of debris in line with its thighs. Black gore showered from those enormous legs and splashed the terrain below, but an otherworldly light had already formed behind those too-human teeth and it grew along with a high-pitched screech coming from the guts of the fiend.

30mm rounds ripped right down the shin of each leg, tearing them apart in uneven halves that crashed to the ground and caused the beast to slam its claws onto the soil to keep itself from toppling over. Two figures arced away from their target as it fell, just as a blinding light erupted from the creature's mouth into the space they left behind. The screech from before was a mouse fart in comparison to the noise of anguish from the dragon, and both Zeke and I grabbed at our ears in a vain attempt to muffle it.

Without Zeke's foot on the gas and his hands on his ears, however, we lost control and veered into the agriculture to our left. He slammed on the brakes by instinct and the truck went into a roll, deploying airbags that did little to cushion the impact of steel on our skulls and bodies. I have no idea how many times the truck rolled, likely twice. Regardless, I ended up with my door against the ground, a flaccid airbag in my face, pain throughout my body, and Zeke dangling above me from his seat belt.

"Zeke!" I knew I was yelling despite the ringing in my ears, not noticing the irony of a deaf person waiting on a response.

I undid my belt, thumped against the window and shifted around to try kicking out the remains of the front windshield. My left arm was broken and it felt like someone had beaten my ribs--probably broken, too--with a bat, but I brought my knees to my chest and heaved against the glass repeatedly until it gave way. I crawled through the opening onto the dirt and hobbled my way back to the road, hugging my left arm to my chest as blood dripped from my head.

The dragon was still bracing itself with its front legs, looking around wildly for the aircraft that had left it crippled, when from above its shoulders I saw two shapes coming to finish their work. Now I looked at its eyes again, knowing the risk but confident in the capabilities of the two pilots who had brought this beast down, and saw a frantic fear where once there was mystic, rapacious glee. The edges of its mouth were drawn down, in a child's scolded frown with tears appearing at the creases of its eyes, but there was another light forming behind the multiple rows of human teeth even as that gigantic head twisted about to try and spot the Warthogs.

Two black fountains erupted behind the monster as its body was torn on either side of the spine by 30mm rounds, and its head flew back in pain. I heard nothing as a bright light spewed out of the dragon's mouth and into the sky. Nothing again as rips formed around the neck and gore darkened the sky. Still nothing as the A-10s zoomed overhead and the corpse smashed the earth, sending a tremor which forced me to the ground as I tried to brace my impact with a broken arm and instead slumped chin-first into the dirt.

The only faculty left to me was my vision, but at that moment, after all I'd been through in the preceding weeks, days, hours and minutes, it was enough. An enormous chin was directly in line with me about a quarter mile up the road, with a slimy purple lip peeled down and a disgusting pink and ulcerous tongue lolling in the dirt beside it. The upper teeth were clamped down around the meat of the tongue with black goo oozing from it, but they were barely exposed against a sagging upper lip. That human nose had the same goo trickling from it also, but to the left and right of it there was open air.

The skull had been split in three different pieces, segmented almost neatly on either side of the nose by the penetrating bullets made possible by the good engineers at General Electric. One ridge of skull was still upright, and on either side dangled an eye socket and accompanying cheekbone. With my chin in the dirt, a smile cracked my lips and despite not being able to hear a sound, I laughed with sadistic mirth, the triumph of survival bringing tears to my eyes.

Suddenly, the two dangling eyes sprang open, focusing directly on me. Nothing else moved on the corpse, but the eyes found mine instantly, shutting me up and filling me with a dread so powerful my lungs ceased their function.

"Sweet flesh, the meat, dripping we take; the bones, marrow we suck," a macabre litany had begun quietly in the back of my mind, unbidden. "Peeling, the skin; shriek, the pain; oozing, the blood; jelly the eyes, we slurp…"

"TRIUMPH?!?" A thousand voices spoke simultaneously over the chants, their pitch and tone all dissimilar and gut-wrenching, "YOU ARE MARKED LIMP ROCK, QUICK SAND FOUNDATION, LEGION MARKED YOU THEN AS NOW. NO RESPITE AWAITS, PEBBLE, YOUR SEED IS MINE JUST SO."

"Tendons stretched, to snap; the joints we gnaw, the blood to drown…"

The eyes slid shut as air filled my lungs, forcing a cough that made my body convulse in pain, but the voices had faded into nothing. I was left there, alone, broken, deaf, but still alive, with the mid-morning sun warming my exposed skin. Painfully, I pushed myself to my feet using my good right hand to balance as I shifted my weight until finally I was upright, and hobbled back to the wreckage of Zeke's truck.

As I came around to the front of the truck and looked into the cab from the hole that used to be the windshield, it was obvious that Zeke was dead. Blood dripped from his dangling head and made a pool on the shattered passenger window. On hands and knees, I dug around for our packs amidst the wreckage. I retrieved them one by one, my hiking backpack and his satchel, and dragged them to the tailgate where I plopped to the ground.

Fishing around in my pack, I pulled out a shirt and clumsily tied it into a sling for my broken arm before pulling out a jar of peanut butter and a water bottle. I braced the water bottle between my knees and twisted off the top with my good hand, when I glanced at Zeke's satchel. The flap was open and there, amidst boxes of ammo and Meals, Ready-to-Eat, was a large red tome edged in gold with a chain around it. With a lock that was now open.

8

In the name of God, the merciful, the compassionate, protector of his followers and defender of the righteous, leaning up against the ruined pickup truck on a dirt road in the middle of the wilderness I felt an odd sense of peace come over me. The stranger's soul had passed easily into God's care, and his expression was no longer of confusion and fear, but of serenity and peace, oblivious to the dashboard that had fused with his lower half. The Twisted One was dead also, and I was alone there, in the dark, resting for a moment as I ate and drank after such a brief but intense moment. Oddly, I felt comfortable there in my solitude.

Dr. Bashir, God rest his soul, had never been the kind of father to hold his daughter's hand, nor do I ever recall him hugging my mother, God rest her soul. Admittedly, my only memories of my mother were more like feelings, warmth and light around a face like mine when I was still a baby. My father explained to me when I was of school age that she had been taken from us in a traffic accident, but I learned later on that it was extremists who had placed a bomb on the side of the road. I learned too that I was in the same car, and that it was only through the grace of God that my tiny body survived an explosion that had destroyed the front half of the vehicle.

There was a room in my father's laboratory where they kept the office supplies, and that is where my earliest memories placed me, watched over by a young woman who answered the telephones and made coffee for the other doctors. Her name was Rund, but I called her Auntie, and she would walk me to the lavatory and give me books to read with pictures of Mickey Mouse and Winnie the Pooh during the day. In the evening time, after she left and the other staff went home to their families, I would sit in the laboratory with my father as he worked at his computer until the sky turned black, when he would close up the building and drive us back to our apartment.

His research and experiments must have been important, because occasionally during the day, important men with nice suits would walk by my closet to meet with him.

"God's peace, sweet Layla!" some said, patting my head or kissing me. "Where is daddy today?"

They disappeared into the laboratory and came out later with my father to attend lunch meetings at the nicest restaurants in the city. My father brought me every time; his way of showing love was to include me in his life, a life that comprised top secret research and lunch meetings with various ministers and government officials. I was happy to sit with my father during those meetings, in the high-backed chairs with the leather seats all in deep brown, seats that dwarfed me and left just my little head peeking above the edge of the table.

We drove in large black sedans with a driver to open the door for us waiting outside the restaurants, always in a group of similar cars, all to escort my father and the important men. When I finally got to attend kindergarten, a similar car picked me up each morning but the driver, Ali, carried a gun on a sling over his shoulder. My father explained to me that because of the political tensions Ali had to carry a gun. I didn't mind because Ali's wife always left a paper bag with dates and bread for me to take to school for lunch.

From kindergarten through middle school, my routine left me very little contact with my father, but every evening he would kiss my cheeks while we shared a dinner that he brought home in Styrofoam boxes and reheated in the microwave oven. Ali picked me up from school early in the morning, took me to ballet or gymnastics after school, and returned me home in the evenings where I did my homework and read Harry

Potter or watched Disney Movies until my father came home. There were always a few attacks each week, news reports of people being killed in the market or on the bus, and I could hear the explosions and police sirens even down my street, but thanks be to God I was never involved with them. More than once, one of the kids wouldn't come to school any more without an explanation, rumors would spread that they were killed in some violent attack, and I would cry a little, alone in the lavatory.

My father told me that our move to America was because in our country, a new government had made it illegal for me to go to high school and college, but I suspected that his research was against the new moral codes that had been forced upon us. I didn't mind either way. It was so exciting to finally get to see New York and California, but he made me promise not to tell my classmates. I'm sure my classmates knew something was up though, because I was giddy all the last week of class when usually I was quiet and shy. I quickly learned that New Mexico is a long way from New York City.

***

It was still quite dark when I packed up my things and left the wreckage to follow that dirt road wherever it took me. I made sure to fasten both knives to my hip before setting off, certain that they should be ready with me now at all times, and prayed again to God to guide my feet on the path to fulfill His righteous designs. With the havoc caused by the Twisted One, I felt that the road was better than the wilderness.

Everything was at peace there on that country road, a night bird made its call and somewhere I heard a wild dog singing in the moonlight. The stars were exceptionally bright with no streetlights to diminish their beauty, and walking beneath such a large moon illuminated my steps almost as well as the sun could but without the heat. Indeed, it was cold after all the hot blood had circulated from me during that frantic moment when survival was all I had, so I hugged myself while placing one foot in front of the next on what seemed a journey with no end.

The moon traversed the sky overhead and a few bats fluttered by in search of their meals when I got another distinct sensation of danger. I thought of Al-Khidr's strange gift then, the one buried deep within my skull during my last revelation, as a prickling began at the top of my neck. Determined to remain calm, I stopped to glance around in the clear night, but I saw nothing as I turned completely around. When I had made one complete turn, though, there directly down the path in front of me was the shape of a man walking towards me. How I had missed him initially while facing that direction I did not know, but there was little doubt in my mind that this was the cause for my newfound caution.

I stood there and said a quiet prayer, which made my muscles relax even though I had not realized they were tense the moment before, and continued forward towards the advancing silhouette. I gripped the hilts of my knives as I strode forward, confident in God's protection. After all, He had just saved me from a beast over thrice my size, so what harm would come to me from a mere human? Each step brought the two of us closer together and I grew ever bolder as I began to recognize the distinct markings of the Faceless.

Suddenly, two sets of strong hands grabbed my wrists from either side and stretched me in opposite directions between them until my feet dangled in the air. The strain at my shoulders was terrible and brought pain as I felt them being torn right from the sockets, the Faceless One advancing on me all the while. I screamed as the pain grew, and I looked to my left into a wet bubble containing all the mysteries of the universe, an image I recognized as the hypnotic power of the Faceless. Fear caught my breath, and I turned to the right to see the same portal to other dimensions staring at me while my shoulders barely held together.

I twisted my wrists and elbows like a belly dancer to escape their grasp, having no other option as I was spread between two Faceless Ones with the third growing closer by the second, his hands directly in front of him as if to strangle me. My right wrist slipped free and I heard a pop as my left arm was pulled from its socket. I fell to the ground with another loud scream. The Faceless One holding my useless left wrist maintained his hold, but the one holding my right had stumbled back upon my surprising release, leaving me pulled to the side by my wrist.

With my left arm held high above my head at an unnatural angle, being disconnected as it was from my shoulder, I used my free hand to grab a knife from my belt. Springing to my feet, I dragged the edge of the knife across the wrists of my captor, severing his tendons and releasing my useless arm to dangle at my side. Using the momentum of that slash to spin myself, I was then looking straight at the Faceless One who had originally held my right arm. I leapt at him, knife held high above my head in a downward stabbing angle, and even as he caught me in a bear hug, I brought my knife down again and again on the cosmos sack that was his face.

He toppled backward as the sack burst and the life fled him, and I rode the corpse to the dirt though a scrambling from behind told me I had yet to defeat the Faceless with the slit wrists. I turned to face him right as the hands of the original fiend latched onto my neck, hauling me to the sky in the same motion and leaving me tip-toed on the corpse of his companion. My vision started to blur and I felt the blood collect in my face while I lashed out with my knife to stab at whatever I could, connecting occasionally with meat.

"Allahu Akbar," I croaked with the remaining breath left in me and brought the edge of my knife skyward, praying to God to connect the tip to that unholy bubble this abomination had in place of a face. I felt the hands release me and I fell against the corpse, rolling to the side slightly away from both monsters. Panting, I pushed myself up with my good hand and saw the Faceless One clutching at his neck where dark liquid was staining his chest and leaking through his fingers.

Clumsy hands tried to grab my limp arm even as I tried to catch my breath. The final Faceless One was upon me.

"Bism Allah al Rahman al Raheem…." I began a litany while slashing back and forth, my limp arm slapping my body as I cut my last assailant to ribbons. When the final monster collapsed, I stood amidst their bodies and screamed at the sky in triumph, blessed in the glory of God's righteous fury.

I wiped my knife on the pants of a Faceless One and returned it to its place on my hip before clutching again at my disconnected arm. Inspiration can take very strange forms when He allows us true insight, because at that moment I remembered watching a movie with my father, God rest his soul, one Thursday evening before the weekend. It was an American film in which two police officers, one white and one black, worked together to stop a kind of drug ring. In the movie, the white officer had his arm disconnected at a crucial time in which some thugs were about to hurt his partner. To fix his arm quickly, the police officer bashed it against a wall until it popped back into place.

With ragged breath, I walked over to a very thick tree a short distance away, confident that if the trick worked for the noble--if destructive--police officer, it would work for me also. I slammed my shoulder into the tree trunk and let out a loud scream again, tears forming in my eyes. I gritted my teeth and tried again. Five times I tried without fixing the issue, and tears were now streaming down my cheeks as I thought hard about how to accomplish the act of mashing my arm back into its socket. Finally, I decided to brace my arm against the tree and squat down quickly to force the socket downward onto the bone. An audible pop told me it had worked, although I dared not move it much for fear it would dislocate again.

A dull orange was starting to permeate my vision as the sun slowly peaked over the horizon, signaling the end of another night of terror. The sky above was all oranges and pinks and reds, gorgeous after the unthinkable night I had lived through, and I said a prayer aloud thanking God for His divine providence. I sat down with my back against that tree and watched the sun rise as if for the first time in all my life, exhausted and broken, with more dried tears on my cheeks but full to the brim with a warmth that I knew came from the light of God.

9

I had a dream once that I was pulling out my own teeth. At first I thought there was something in my mouth, so I pushed my thumb and forefinger against the molars there on the top row. One of my teeth just felt off. It was rough and didn't at all feel like my tooth. I grasped it and shook it slightly, feeling just how loose it was and then I gave it a tug.

Excruciating pain shot up the side of my face like a spider web beneath my skin, all through the temple and up to the crown of my head, but I just kept pulling at it. Finally the tooth broke free, but it was connected by an infinitely long nerve which I felt slide from inside my cranium all the way out of the bloody gap I'd created in my own mouth.

I repeated the process once more, until in front of me on the tablecloth were two teeth covered in mouth slime, blood and nerves. The teeth reminded me of seeds, their nerves the roots, and even as I thought that the nerves began burrowing into the tablecloth ripping the cotton thread. They bored madly into the wood of the table, squirming through the air between the table and into the earth below. The seed-teeth then began to grow, not into the trees I had expected, but into fetuses.

Two identical fetuses with their umbilical cords connected directly to the earth were growing at an alarming rate on the red-and-white checkered tablecloth in front of me. Without an amniotic sac in which to grow, their alien-bodies flopped about on the table like salmon on the deck of a boat until the fin-looking appendages grew into proper limbs. They continued to mature before me from zygote to infant to toddler, until finally they pushed up on their own and stood, two identical little boys. Their hair was brown and shaggy, their skin pale and covered in slime. They were almost perfect replicas of me with one exception.

Their eyes were enormous, a blue so deep I could not imagine any other color, so familiar my mind focused on them entirely like trying to remember an old song. There were other colors there too: yellow, white, purple and green, all moving...

***

I remember sweat dripping all over my body as I shot bolt upright in bed. My hands felt around for Lindsay in the dark, but she was gone. Just then, light flooded the room as the bathroom door came open. With the light behind her, all I could see was her shadow, her left hand raised and holding something.

"I'm pregnant, Pete."

***

I blinked away the memory, my brain slipping in and out of the present, and took a sip of water from the bottle in my good hand. Swallowing hurt. Not as much as breathing of course, but since I didn't have any Motrin nearby, the only other cure-all I had was water. I fumbled the bottle when I tried to set it down, spilling the last of my water over my thigh, and leaned back against the sideways tailgate of Zeke's old Toyota.

My head lolled to the side. It had grown exceptionally heavy, leading my eyes back to that red and gold tome still sitting in the old satchel. I wiped my brow with my "good" hand and slowly pulled the book out of the bag. The chains fell away as I pulled it out and onto my lap, my legs barely noticing the weight of such a heavy volume, and I pried open the cover.

A cloud of dust came out from beneath the cover and the pages, which made me cough as it tickled my nose. Specks of blood flew from my mouth with each successive cough, and my ribs were on fire with the uncontrollable muscle movements which forced pain up and down my spine. My vision blurred, and I clamped my eyes shut until the pain receded. When I opened them again, I was staring at a blank page with just a few new red specks.

I turned the page. Blank.

I turned the page again. Blank again.

I flipped page after page after page of blank paper. Blood loss and shock must have made me delirious, because I started laughing. I flipped innumerable pages, cackling like a fiend, until I coughed up a huge blob of blood all over the pages in front of me. I put my hand over my mouth to prevent more blood from soaking through but there was too much and it dripped from between my fingers and onto the red-covered page.

A sudden blast of wind to my face forced my head against the truck and I started to swoon. Leaves battered my face along with the choppy wind, but I opened my eyes against it as best I could, prepared to be eaten by some gigantic beast since that was the most likely thing to happen at any given moment now.

From my slit eyes, I saw a Blackhawk's open door spewing uniformed men with guns. I couldn't hear a thing, but their mouths were open and they were gesturing in my direction even as I fell to my side in a heap. Through slow blinks, I watched them advance on me, but my eyes got distracted when they glanced at the open book I'd just covered in blood.

Peeking through the blood, letters started to fade into focus as if the blood itself was turning into red ink before my delirious eyes. The last thing I saw before rough hands grabbed my shoulders and the world went black was blood-ink with the words:

In the name of God, the merciful and just, my dreams prior to my first day of American school were so vivid that there shall be no error when I recount them here, such were the dreams granted to me by God that night, some of which have already come to pass, and some of which I should pray in His Holy Name should never befall this Earth, for if they should indeed begin here not a one amongst us who has yet to turn towards God shall be united in the glorious kingdom of heaven.

10

In the name of God, the merciful and just, benevolent peace bringer, ruler of all creation, the sense of peace I felt underneath the shade of His tree in the middle of the wilderness was more profound than anything I had felt up to that moment. My shoulder throbbed dully, but even that persistent pain could not diminish the luster of God's precious sun as it dispelled the darkness from the direction of His blessed city. Indeed, the sun's rays penetrated my skin deeply and warmed my very soul with the peace He granted me after the terrors of the night.

I broke my fast then, after offering my thanks in prayer to God above, still seated against the rough wood of the desert tree. It was His design to offer me this peace, so I honored Him by using it to collect my thoughts and assemble the various experiences I'd lived through into a cohesive plan. The gem sitting at the bottom of my backpack was quite powerful, but that power was in some way linked to Iblis.

The gem seemed to have the ability to add its corruption to the minds and shapes of whatever beasts were nearby. In the case of the cow, elongated horns, sharpened and jagged teeth, increased speed, and of course aggression were the manifestations of the gem's corruption, and I shuddered to think of what would happen to an already ferocious beast. Would, for example, a tiger be granted increased strength, even longer teeth and claws, and speed to rival an automobile? The Twisted Ones would be my primary concern when handling the gem.

The gem's power to twist beasts seemed limited to those within the immediate vicinity, as in the case of my father, God rest his soul, I had encountered no such djinn. Although of that I could not be certain, since the change that had occurred within the cow coincided with nightfall, and I had fled the scene of my father's death before such time.

Faceless Ones posed an even larger conundrum though, because I could not be entirely certain whether or not my father, God rest his soul, had indeed revealed the gem. The Faceless were abnormally strong but did not hurry in their movements, which in my estimation was due to their reliance on the undeniable ability of hypnotism they possessed. They did, however, appear quite suddenly and without warning or indication of their place of origin. Did they possess human hosts and then walk towards the gem, or did they somehow alter the fabric of space and time to appear in distant locations? They could have been following me since my initial encounter at my house, plodding along until they found me in the desert.

I shuddered at the thought of thousands of Faceless pushing towards me even now, and unconsciously grabbed the hilts of my knives. Comforted by the twin blades, I realized that regardless of their number they were vulnerable to conventional destruction, as were the Twisted. I also took comfort in knowing that their hypnosis did not affect me any longer, though I wondered at the reasoning. Was I alone immune to their power, due to my encounter with Al-Khidr, or was it because I had lived through the initial encounter with a dying Faceless One? Would, for example, any other human be rendered immune after surviving their entrancing gaze?

Unsatisfied with such musings, I turned my focus to the gem itself. I was absolutely certain that it was a creation of Iblis, if not a piece of his own body. Since it was quite obvious that it was a creation or embodiment of pure evil, my primary concern over the object was how it came to be in my father's possession.   I recalled him mentioning a kind of electromagnetic spectrum experiment he had conducted, but I was stymied as to how that would translate into the terrible gem. Was he perhaps testing the gem itself, or was it the byproduct of some experiment?

I took a drink of water to dispel the thoughts from my mind, unwilling to accept that it was my father, God rest his soul, who had unleashed such a blight on the world. Instead, I pondered Al-Khidr and his strange gift. It was placed within my brain, the memory still quite vivid of his hands prying my skull apart to deposit it therein, and he had mentioned the senses. He alluded to more than those with which I was familiar: touch, taste, smell, hearing, and sight.

I was immune to the hypnosis of Faceless, I'd been able to outrun the Twisted One, and even as I thought about it, my arm was healing much faster than I'd assumed possible. Saying a prayer of thanks to God, with a special mention for Al-Khidr, I stood up and gathered my things.

My contemplation had bolstered my spirits, and the thought that God Himself guided my steps reassured me. I decided in that moment that since there was nothing left for me of the life I had once desired (school, friends, work, love), I would strive to use the gift of God to undo the wrong that I carried on my back. I would either find a way to destroy that demon gem, or I would hide it away for all time.

Thinking back on how the gem had responded when revealed to the light of day, I resolved to take it to a place it would not be discovered. Picturing in my mind the map of the world we had studied so long ago in school, I promised God that I would lock it away in His frozen tundra to the north. With the morning sun to my right, I started walking.

ACT 2

11

"We're all fine, Pete. The boys are just playing with their iPads." Lindsay's voice came out ragged over the phone. "I'm just wondering why we're down here over some sunspots."

"Better safe than sorry, love." The connection wasn't good but Pete's concern was audible. "It just doesn't make sense, you know? I mean it's Seattle! This city runs off the internet. Put Billy on, okay?"

Lindsay walked across the room to where William sat on the couch, his eyes fixed on the dinosaur on the iPad who was crushing houses and cars. She pushed the phone in front of the iPad, thumbing the speaker button.

"Billy?"

"Uh-huh." William was steering the dinosaur into an airport. "Dad, I just crushed a jet!"

"That's great, son. Listen, I love you, okay? Be good for mom and I'll meet up with you soon, okay?"

"Okay, Dad."

"I love you. Let me talk to your brother."

Lindsay carried the phone across the living room, around the coffee table and held it by Theo's head.

"Theo? Teddy? It's your dad!"

"Daddy!" the four year old squealed, looking up from a YouTube video of a woman with an Indian accent singing nursery rhymes. "Daddy, grandpa's dog licked me and I punched him. I don't like that dog, daddy."

"Oh no! Okay, listen. You be a good boy, okay? Listen to momma, okay?"

"Okay, dad. Love you."

"I love you. Goodnight."

Lindsay thumbed the speaker phone button and brought the phone to her ear.

"Sweetheart," the concern was still there, but Pete sounded calm now, "I love you so much."

"Yeah, yeah. Love you too."

"Lindsay? Hey, I put the pistol under the driver's seat--just listen," he spoke over her anticipated protests. "I don't know what's going on, but just remember: pull back on the top part, point at what you want to die, and squeeze the trigger. There isn't a safety on a Sig, so be certain you're ready. There is a magazine in it already and one in the box."

"Jesus, Pete." A headache was already growing right behind her eyes with every word he spoke. "What the Hell is wrong with you?"

"I love you. I'll talk to you soon. Goodnight."

"Love you."

Lindsay set her phone down on the coffee table and plopped down next to Theodore on the couch. It was nine o'clock, but with all the excitement Pete had caused pushing them out of the house in such a hurry, the kids were nowhere near ready for sleep. She let them zone out on their games and massaged her temples, trying to relax with the notion of a loaded gun sitting in the Toyota Sienna parked outside her father's two-story Gresham house.

This was the first time Pete had ever gone so far as to kick her and the kids out based on some wild doomsday notion, but he was definitely in the habit of taking his paranoia to the extreme. She recalled the time he kicked in the door, one hand holding a stopwatch, the other holding a bullhorn. He was shouting obscenities as the kids started running around in a panic, their tiny hands holding their ears, while all she could do was cross her hands over her chest and shake her head. Eventually, he stopped yelling and commenced some droning speech about thugs, terrorists, and looters.

The kids went crazy for the excitement, brainstorming about hiding under the bed or running to the closet upstairs. Lindsay, on the other hand, made certain to lecture Pete thoroughly about how unproductive such an exercise was if she herself had no prior knowledge. They spent a couple hours hashing out the details of what to do in case an armed extremist burst into the house, intent on terrorizing one small family in the suburbs of Seattle. He repeated the exercise twice more. Although she would never admit it, Lindsay was glad to have some plan and extremely proud at how calmly and quickly a five-year-old and a four-year-old were trained to react.

As she sat on the couch, listening to that cheery Indian woman sing "London Bridge", Lindsay shivered with a dread she could only attribute to her husband of nine years' sudden reaction. She put her elbows on her knees and let her head fall into her hands, closing her eyes tightly against the coming tears, thankful she hadn't cut those bangs into her shoulder-length brown hair for fear of further worrying her two children.

Thankfully, too, her father, had agreed to let her and the boys come down on short notice. He was with his wife Lorie on vacation in Las Vegas at the time, but was all too eager to have his only grandchildren mess up his house while he was away. His only condition was that they stay for the duration of the conference plus two days, as he wanted to take young Willie to the museum upon his return.

They were set up in the basement of the two story home in Gresham, Oregon. It was a quiet area, though growing steadily, and her father's house was set on just under an acre, with fruit trees, a well-manicured garden maintained by Grammy Lorie, and surrounded by a tall chain-link fence. Poncho Villa, the family mutt, roamed the grounds outside, completing patrol after patrol, disturbed by the sudden arrival of the little people.

"Okay, boys, five more minutes," Lindsay said, more composed than she felt at the moment. Non-committal grunts from both boys let her know that at least some part of their subconscious had registered a noise from her general area. She walked back through the laundry/living room towards the bedroom to lay out pajamas for the kids, but stopped at the door. She really didn't want a loaded pistol in the van. She didn't want it in the house either, but she definitely wanted immediate access to it in her heightened state of anxiety.

"Well, turn them off when I come back from the van, okay?" More grunts, but Lindsay continued up the stairs leading from the basement to the side door. She was still dressed in jeans and a hoodie from the ride up, so she slipped on some low-top sneakers and walked out into the night. Poncho was moving around somewhere on the other side of the house. She could hear him trotting towards her as her feet crunched gravel on the way to the van.

"What's up, Poncho?" she said as he made his way around the corner with his mouth hanging open. "Everything cool?" His head went instinctively towards her outstretched hand while she maintained her path towards the driver seat. Although he was more than welcome in the house, Poncho preferred the outdoors, possibly because his long tail was beyond control in a house crowded with old World War 2 books and miniatures, possibly because he could roll in dirt and eat the fermented apples after they had sat on the ground for too long.

The Sienna beeped when Lindsay disarmed the alarm and opened the door. Sure enough, there was the pistol box right underneath the driver's seat. She opened the thin plastic box to check on the contents, then quickly closed it, shut the door, and went back inside. Poncho waited by the van, sniffing the dirt and milling about before making his way over to the eaves of the garage to lay down on the filthy tarp he called bed.

"Okay, boys, put 'em up!" she called down even before she slid the deadbolt to the backdoor and walked down the creaky stairs. A chorus of moans greeted her at the landing, but they complied nonetheless. Lindsay shepherded the boys into the bedroom where they stripped down. Willie pulled on his Scooby Doo jammies, but Theo still required some help with the long-sleeved fish jammies he couldn't sleep without.

"Let's go pee-pee boys. Come on."

"It's 'piss' mom," Theo said, chin in the air and hands on his hips. "That's what dad calls it."

"And 'dump,' " Will added.

"Well, go take a piss then!" Lindsay threw her free hand up in exasperation, strangling Pete in her mind for any number of reasons. She put the gun box in the top of the closet as the boys ran off towards the bathroom, pushing one another and crowding around the toilet to pee in tandem. Their little boy aim was off, and they ended up splashing on the seat and over the edge, but that was something Lindsay had given up worrying about long ago. She kept one of the tidiest houses she knew of, outside of her online friends whose husbands' work allowed for nannies and maid services, but even Lindsay Macintosh could do very little for the smell of urine in her boys' bathroom.

She was reminded of something she'd seen online where a mom put stickers of jungle beasts and apes in the bottom of the toilet to encourage good aim. Making a mental note to look it up after the kids were sleeping, Lindsay ushered the boys into the bedroom and onto the blow-up mattress with the floral quilt. Lindsay didn't care that they were bouncing. She could ignore that, and the noise was a nice distraction from the script she was developing in her mind to use on Pete when she saw him next.

"Enough boys, it's late now." She walked over and switched off the overhead light. "Let's just settle down." Squatting down, she kissed them on their heads. "Sweet dreams."

With that, she plugged in her phone and lay down on the bed across the room from the air mattress. She started asking around in her forums and groups about the toilet stickers, but her eyes were getting increasingly heavy. With an effort, Lindsay got out of bed, peeled off her jeans, put on some pajama pants, then went out to the bathroom to brush and get ready for sleep.

***

The sky was a swirling tornado, clouds of green and purple, twisting disturbingly in both directions as Lindsay Macintosh looked out from the top of the hill down on the sprawling metropolis below. Faster and faster they spun, until a drill of clouds formed pointing directly at the heart of the city. Buildings, streets, trees--everything the clouds touched was pulled up from the roots and thrown into the sky. She blinked and was downtown, looking straight up into the funnel of twisting steel and concrete ripped from the earth with the tornado's power. With that nauseating swirl of clouds raging all around her, she grasped the sides of her head between her hands and looked directly at the ground.

She stood on the exposed dirt that lay beneath I-5, but the Earth was scarred and oozing black. Worms pushed their way through the surface, writhing as though poisoned by the black slime flowing along up from unknown depths. From the dark brown soil, two hands pushed their way to the surface. The nails were crusted with the filth and debris of digging through a compost bin. Black showed from underneath the fingernails and there was a stink like rotten meat stuck to the bottom of a garbage can.

The hands were much larger than any human hands, with knuckles easily two feet across, and they kept clawing and digging at the dirt in a rush to break out. Lindsay backed away, still clutching the sides of her head, until her back bumped against something solid. She turned to see a grey forearm about the size of a tanker car connected to a fist larger than two Volkswagen buses. Her head followed the forearm all the way up an equally large bicep to a shoulder. Just above the shoulder was the underside of chin, dripping fluid down to splash the earth around her in drops the size of cattle.

Suddenly, the chin dropped down, with two enormous slug-like lips parting into a cruel sneer. The teeth behind those purple, slick lips were hideous, yellow and jagged. The breath that escaped from between them sickened Lindsay until vomit came from her mouth. Even as she emptied her stomach, her eyes remained locked upward, past that sadistic grin, past the hairy nostrils...

Lindsay's hands dropped to her side, vomit dripping down the front of her chest and onto the ground, and her mouth dropped open. Hundreds of feet above her, two blue eyes darker than the Mariana Trench focused on her, gluing her to the ground. They started getting closer, revealing splashes of yellow and orange at the edges, pinpricks of light coming through like holes in a blue sheet with a lamp behind it. She was stuck there as that gargantuan head drew ever closer. With her gaze stuck on those eyes, she barely noticed the heat wave coming from the creature's mouth. The breath felt like a sulfuric hot spring, steaming her face and body, but it hardly registered as important when she was about to see the inside of the universe.

An intense vibration started in her skull, and she grabbed at her ears to shut it out, wrenching her eyes away from the hypnotic trance. Her vision grew shaky as the vibration increased in frequency and volume. The sound grew so loud that Lindsay could not think or move, it was all-encompassing; the world went black.

***

Lindsay's eyes shot open, looking for the source of that terrible buzzing. She propped herself up on her elbows, noticing the glow from the face of her smart phone on the windowsill. She scrambled towards the blinking light, feeling something wet on the comforter on the bed beside her, and frantically mashed the face until the buzzing stopped. She shined the screen onto the surface of the bed, revealing chunks of half-digested food and yellow bile. The mess was not limited to the blankets, however. There were bits of stomach juice and food on her chin and chest, too.

Swearing under her breath, she wiped her chin with the back of her hand and turned the phone over, letting the light hit her eyes directly.

She blinked at the new message icon in the system tray at the top of the screen, hoping for news from Pete. When her eyes finally focused, she dropped the phone into the pile of vomit on the bed.

The screen displayed a message from the Wireless Emergency Alerts system:

THE CITY OF SEATTLE, WA IS CURRENTLY UNDER ATTACK BY AN UNKNOWN SOURCE. ALL RESIDENTS ARE ADVISED TO SHELTER IN PLACE, LOCK ALL DOORS AND WINDOWS, AND REMAIN CALM. LAW ENFORCEMENT AGENCIES AND THE DEPARTMENT OF DEFENSE WILL REPORT TO THEIR STATIONS AND/OR MILITARY INSTALLATIONS IMMEDIATELY. A NATIONAL STATE OF EMERGENCY HAS BEEN DECLARED.

12

"All available assets have been deployed to combat this new threat. At this time, we have not determined the source of the threat, but let me be clear: an attack on American citizens on American soil will be punished immediately and decisively. I ask all Americans to remain vigilant and prepared to defend themselves and their families. God Bless America."

"We turn now to our Senior Military Analyst, Retired General Jason Coupler." The reporter looked fresh even in the middle of the night. "Mr. Coupler, when the President says 'all available assets' what exactly is he talking about? I mean, this is an attack on Seattle itself."

"Yes, Joint Base Lewis-McChord is less than 30 miles south of Seattle proper, so we can assume that each of the maneuver units have responded already: 1st Special Forces Group, 2nd Ranger Battalion, not to mention the Air Force Wings. Don't forget Everett Naval Station, the Coast Guard. Whoever this is made a huge miscalculation when they decided to attack the Pacific Northwest."

Lindsay pressed the "mute" button and walked away from the couch. The world outside the window in the living room was black. She stood at the window, arms crossed across her vomit-crusted chest, and stared out into the darkness. Every five minutes for the last two hours, she'd called, texted, and private messaged Pete, but he wasn't responding. Her eyes were sore from crying, and she could tell by the numbness in her arms and stomach that she had entered a mild state of shock.

Her eyes suddenly focused on the image reflected in the glass, and Lindsay was brought back to the present by the crusted filth covering her body. She shuddered, and walked past the kitchen back to the stairs leading to the basement. She couldn't shake the feeling that her family was no longer safe and that Pete wouldn't be coming back to protect them. With only the light streaming in from upstairs, she made her way through the dark basement apartment to the bedroom.

Both kids were still asleep, miraculously, so she rummaged as quietly as possible in the suitcase for a change of clothes. Her hands groped in the dark and bumped into the gun case. The President's words echoed in her mind:

"I ask all Americans to remain vigilant and prepared to defend themselves and their families."

Lindsay tucked the plastic box under her arm and gathered fresh clothes in her hands. There was a bathroom downstairs, but she didn't want to risk waking the boys, so she set the clean clothes on the couch along with the gun. Shrouded in darkness, Lindsay returned to the bedroom to strip the linens and soiled comforter from the bed. She stood in front of the washing machine, stripped off her dirty clothes, and dumped the whole mess of fabric and stomach contents into the machine.

After retrieving the bundle of clothes from the couch, Lindsay walked in a trance up the stairs to the main floor of her father's house. From the top of the stairs she could see a live feed of Seattle shot from a hillside, some miles from the city proper. Fire spewed from every window of the once picturesque skyline. Bricks and steel rained down from the tallest buildings. Lindsay gasped as airplanes streaked across the sky, loosing bombs as they made a pass over the city, creating more chaos and debris.

The camera shook with the impact of multiple bombs striking deep within the city, and Lindsay couldn't watch any more. She continued on towards the bathroom, trying to keep her mind off her husband caught somewhere north in the midst of all that chaos. With the warm water running she relaxed a little, but nothing could shake the fear she felt in her heart that her best friend, the father of her children, was dead or injured and definitely alone. Tears mixed with warm water as she stood, sobbing with the fear of loss but finally able to focus on her family's situation.

Eager to be close to her beloved sons, Lindsay cut her shower short, toweled dry, and then wrapped her hair up in the towel as she pulled on her underwear and yoga pants. Suddenly, Poncho started barking and growling from outside. Mixed with the growling was a shuffling of feet and a sudden grunt, and then the unmistakable squeal of a beaten dog accompanied by whimpers. Panic welled up in Lindsay's gut as her shaky hands went for the plastic gun case on their own.

She didn't feel the Sig's sand-paper grip in her trembling hand. Her actions were rushed and frantic as she heard the distinctive sound of glass shattering from the basement. She tripped at the top of the stairs, smacking against them but continuing towards the bedroom.

"Mommy?" Billie's groggy voice came from the bedroom, followed by a scream. The scream was cut short, however, and replaced quickly by choking noises.

Lindsay pushed herself to her feet, ignoring the pain spreading from her left elbow which had taken the brunt of her fall. She burst through the door onto a scene out of a nightmare.

A hooded figure had William's throat grasped between both hands, William's hands were grasping the figure's wrists as his little feet drummed against the torso. Brave Theo was just waking up and screamed loud at the horror in front of him. Lindsay registered all of this in a split second. Before the gravity had time to sink in, she was crashing into the hooded figure from the side.

The attacker broke Lindsay's fall as they smashed into the cement wall of the basement. With a ferocity borne of panic and fear for her son's life, she smashed the barrel of the pistol into that hooded face. With the force of impact and the pistol's steel crushing his face, the attacker released Willie, who collapsed into a heap on the floor. Lindsay didn't stop with the first blow, however. She repeatedly struck at the face as fluid splashed across her and the rest of the basement. She couldn't feel her arms or body at all, just the vibrations radiating from her hand that shook her teeth with the force of each strike.

Small hands grabbed her around the waist, and she spun around to see Theo's eyes grown large in the dark at the sight of mommy bludgeoning the attacker to death in front of him.

"Mommy..." She spared a moment for him before turning swiftly towards William, who lay on the floor coughing and whimpering.

Lindsay dropped the gun and scooped up his body, clutching him to her chest and rocking gently. She pulled Theodore close too, and kissed both their heads while they sobbed into her chest.

For the first time in her life, huddled there in the dark with what remained of her family, Lindsay Macintosh prayed.

13

Lindsay Macintosh held her children as tightly as she could, not willing to let them go even when they grunted from the pressure. Somewhere outside, a sound from Poncho reminded her of where she was: in the basement of her father's house with her kids and the corpse of an attacker.

"Come on, boys." She managed to hide the fear she felt with a motherly confidence. "Let's go upstairs."

The trio untangled, but the boys didn't want to leave their mother's side, not even when she stooped down to retrieve the handgun she'd used as a bludgeon moments earlier. They made their way in the dark up the stairs to the family room, where the muted television was showing more live footage of the war zone that their former home had become. A news anchor stood far away from an artillery piece, gesturing towards it with one hand while holding a microphone in the other; the picture shook and he dropped the microphone to clamp both hands on his ears.

Fire came from the huge gun as it rocked backwards with the force of the blast. The crew reloaded it and fired again. The camera panned to a shot of the city, where a building collapsed under the impact of the barrage. The scene was still blurry, despite the fires burning throughout the city helping to illuminate the destruction, but there were large shadows moving through the city. The camera man caught a shadowy movement for a moment and zoomed in.

"Is that the new Godzilla, Mommy?" Theodore, obsessed with dinosaurs, asked.

Lindsay squinted at the television, unable to believe what she saw. The blurry outline of some type of creature was climbing onto the remains of a building, its long arms and legs propelling it quickly from the ground. A white light formed in what appeared to be the creature's mouth. Suddenly, the screen went white. A message flashed on-screen about technical difficulties, but was quickly replaced by two stunned studio anchors, their mouths agape.

Snatching up the remote, Lindsay switched the TV off. She had seen so much within the last few hours that her brain couldn't handle a Japanese monster destroying the Emerald City. She ushered the boys into the kitchen and took the towel hanging from the oven door to wipe her kids up. With the light on them, she noticed the fluid all over her and Willie was clear and came off easily with the towel. She had assumed it was blood earlier, which made her heart stop with the thought that the attacker downstairs was just unconscious.

"Willie, can you pour some milk for your little brother? He's a little shaken up. I'm going to get some clothes from downstairs."

"Momma, no! The bad guy is down there! Don't leave!" he shrieked.

"It's okay, baby." She lifted the gun. "I've got daddy's gun. Just stay up here with your brother."

Tears formed at the corners of his eyes, but he nodded and hugged his brother, who let out a croak.

She kissed their heads and lifted the gun to shoulder level. This time, she remembered to cock the weapon before turning on the ceiling lights in the stairwell.

"Hold the gun to your chest, between your boobs like this." Pete's voice echoed in her head. "Keep two hands on it. They hold the gun out in front in the movies, but if you are in a tight space and you intend to kill someone, this way is better. I mean, if your gun is the first thing to pop around the corner, they can grab your wrists. If they try and grab your body, all you have to do is pull the trigger."

She pulled the gun to her chest and descended the staircase, careful not to make a sound. Moving silently on the old staircase proved challenging, however, so she tried to stay to the outside of the steps, avoiding the worn inside. She held her breath almost the entire time, worried that even the slightest noise would awaken whoever was in the basement. Pausing at each step made the short flight seem infinite, but eventually she reached the laundry/family room.

Nobody jumped out at her. Nobody ran towards her. She was entirely alone.

Lindsay crept to the bedroom, giving the door a wide berth with the expectation that just behind the door was a murderer waiting for her. Not daring to take her hands away from the pistol grip, she didn't bother turning on the light in the bedroom. There in the corner was the crumpled shape of a human being. With small, quiet steps, Lindsay Macintosh moved towards the body fully expecting it to jump up at her.

There was no rise or fall to the chest, no twitch of muscle, no indication of life at all from the body. Dumbfounded, Lindsay kicked it with her foot and jumped back, prepared for the assault she could sense. She tried again, with the same response. She was confused then, and needed final answers, so she walked over to the light switch and flipped it on.

The man was much bigger than she'd originally suspected. Even curled up against the wall he took up almost as much space as the full-sized air mattress. His clothing was unremarkable: jeans, grey hoodie, plain black running shoes. Nothing to mark him as a soldier or linked to the assault on Seattle in any way. Lindsay thought he may be an opportunist, a looter intent on capitalizing on the chaos to the north.

With her right hand on the Sig, held as far into her right shoulder as she could allow, Lindsay slowly pulled the hood off her assailant's head. Her grip on the pistol tightened as she looked at the mutilated remains of a human face. The skin was peeled entirely off the head but instead of solid bone beneath, there was just the raw meat of a brain and a nasal cavity. The forehead had been sheared away along with the nose, but the cheek bones and jaw remained, though they were covered in blood and gore. A slimy pool had formed on the cement floor and streaks of the same mucus dripped from the walls.

Lindsay's breath caught in her throat and she backed away from the body, one hand over her mouth, the other still pointing the gun. When she cleared the doorway, she ran back up the stairs and into the kitchen, where she found spilt milk on the floor and two little boys hugging each other while drinking their milk. The sight of her two children huddled together on the floor, visibly shaking with fright, forced tears to the corners of her eyes.

"It's going to be okay." Lindsay hugged them both. "We're all going to be okay."

"I miss Daddy. Where is Daddy?" Theo asked, his small hands in a death grip on the plastic mug of milk.

New tears streamed from her eyes and onto her children's heads, but she choked back the sobs to keep some confidence in her voice.

"I'm going to call the police now, okay?" She pushed away slightly from the boys and walked over to the couch to retrieve her cell phone. "How about some cartoons? Willie, why don't you get it set up?"

Theodore ran for the couch, his worries temporarily forgotten, and climbed over the back of the couch to plop down on the middle cushion. Willie was all sniffles, but obediently retrieved the remote and turned on Netflix. Lindsay dialed in the three numbers she had long since memorized but never had a need to use.

For three minutes, Lindsay stood watching SpongeBob while the telephone rang. Although she had never used the service before, she was astounded to wait for such a long period of time.

"9-1-1, what is the location of your emergency?"

"215 Southeast Ross Way, Gresham."

"What is your name?"

"Lindsay Macintosh."

"What is the nature of your emergency?"

"Someone broke into the house and tried to kill my son, so I fought him. Now he's dead in the basement."

"Okay, lock your doors and windows, ma'am, and we'll get someone out there as soon as we can."

"Sure. How long will that be? My kids and I are all alone here."

"Look, Ms. ..."

"Macintosh."

"Ms. Macintosh, yes. Is everyone safe there?"

"Well..."

"If nobody is hurt or injured, we don't have anyone to spare. I have your information in the system, so someone will be over to assist you as soon as possible. "

"Okay, are you going to stay on the line with me until someone gets here?"

The only response she got was a dial tone. Lindsay shook her head. The surreal nature of all the things that had happened within less than 24 hours made her suddenly exhausted. She walked towards the kitchen and set the Keurig for one large cup. While the machine worked, Lindsay pulled up her contacts list and absently thumbed through the names, trying to think of someone who would be able to make it over and help her with the kids.

Most of her friends had moved away or had families of their own. Even though they might be close by, they were probably worried about the events in Seattle. Pete's parents had moved to Arizona the previous year, and her brother was living in Salem still with a girl he met over the internet. The sound of coffee pouring told her she needed some milk, so she left the phone on the counter and retrieved the whole milk from the refrigerator.

She pulled the full cup from under the Keurig, added a little milk, and returned the carton to the refrigerator. The coffee helped clear her head, so she picked up her phone and searched her contacts one last time, confident that there was still one person in the city she could call on for help. With a little caffeine in her system, she analyzed the realities she was faced with, though they were almost ridiculous enough for her to break out in laughter.

With her husband caught in the middle of World War 3 (possibly dead and definitely alone), and a mutilated, faceless corpse in the basement, there was only one person in the Portland Metro area she could trust with her family's safety…if he was sober tonight.

14

"Uh-huh," a voice mumbled on the other end of Lindsay Macintosh's phone.

"Steve! Steve, wake up!"

"Hmm. Who is this?"

"Steve, it's Lindsay. Steve, listen, wake up!"

"Lindsay?"

"Yeah Lindsay Macintosh. Pete's wife? We've known each other for like, seven years?"

"Oh, yeah." She could hear him struggling to get to a seated position. "Lindsay, it's…early. What's up?"

"Yeah, you have my dad's address, right?"

"Out in Gresham? No, but I remember where it is."

"Good. Listen, Steve. We need you out here right away."

"What? Why?"

"Turn on the TV Steve. Pete's in Seattle and we had a break-in here."

"Did you call the cops?"

"Steve, just get here, will ya?"

"Okay, yeah. I'm up."

"Bye." Lindsay hung up quickly and carried her coffee back into the family room where the two boys were sitting next to one another holding hands. Their milk cups were balanced on the unoccupied couch cushions to their left and right, which would have upset Pete. Just thinking of him was enough to make her heart beat quickly with worry.

She moved the empty cups to a television tray next to the couch and pushed her way between the two little boys on the couch. They were watching the episode of SpongeBob Square Pants where SpongeBob and Patrick were depicted as cavemen. The boys chuckled occasionally at their favorite parts, which gave Lindsay a sense of relief after all the events of the last few hours. Knowing Steve would arrive in an hour or so was also relieving, though she anticipated an awkward reunion.

Steve Owens was an old friend of Pete's who, like so many Army veterans, had gotten out of the military without any plan or care. He was the kind of veteran who desperately needed the structure of service but couldn't stand the notion of someone structuring his life for him. He now spent all his time drinking and writing angry letters to senators, congressmen, newspapers, anarchist groups, communists, etc.

He was a great guy, but the last time Lindsay saw him was at a Thanksgiving dinner where he got drunk and tried peeing in her father's kitchen sink. Lindsay was furious but Pete reminded her that it by far wasn't the worst place he could have peed. That didn't stop Lindsay from berating him and kicking him out of her father's house. That was three years ago. Pete occasionally gave her updates on Steve, letting her know that he wasn't just a bum and that he was really sorry. When Lindsay asked if he was still living in his old RV surrounded by guns, beer cans and pornography, Pete was always bashful.

Sipping coffee with her boys watching cartoons seemed so normal she was able to distance herself from all the madness. She found herself laughing at Caveman Squidward, and finally noticed how sore her arm was from punching the bad guy repeatedly. She rubbed at her shoulder with her free hand, then walked across the room to the cabinet where her dad kept the Ibuprofen. She chased two Ibuprofen with coffee and plopped down onto the couch once more.

"Mommy," Willie asked, "was that bad man dead?"

Lindsay paused. "Yes, he's dead."

Willie tilted his head, thinking about the implications of a dead man in the basement with his six-year-old mind.

"He was choking me though, right?"

"Yeah."

"Thanks for saving me, Mom."

Lindsay set her coffee on the floor and squeezed her little boy, then pulled back and grabbed little Theo in her embrace as well. Without warning, the glass door leading to the deck shuddered with the force of fists slamming into it. Lindsay stood and whirled around to see what was going on, while another hooded attacker slammed his fists and forearms against the door.

"Run! Get upstairs, NOW!"

The boys screamed and started running frantically for the stairs, but another pounding sound came from the front door, which was on the way to the staircase. Theo ran upstairs, but Willie just stood there, staring at the little window in the front door. Meanwhile, Lindsay ran for the kitchen to grab the Sig that she had left on the stove moments ago. She grabbed it and caught sight of William standing and staring at the front door.

"Willie," she shook him. "Get up those stairs and help your brother..."

She followed his gaze to the front door, where the attacker was making every attempt to bash through. In the small window of glass, Lindsay and William both saw a slick pool of water containing tiny lights like little stars attached to the neck of a human being. Something within the sack swirled and a small cloud of phosphorescent dust surfaced, like watching a star being born. There were dull thuds occasionally coming from somewhere far off, the sound coming through as though muffled and through a tunnel.

Theodore, came down the stairs to find Lindsay and William standing in front of the door, their heads cocked to the side, looking at those mystic lights dancing continuously in that perfect sphere of a face in front of them.

"Mommy?" Theo was screaming between tears. He ran up to his mother and threw his arms around her neck. "Mommy, they're coming!"

She shook her head, seeing him for the first time, just as the sound of shattering glass told her the door to the patio had finally broken. Shaking her head again to get the strange image of an unknown portion of the galaxy out of her head, Lindsay pushed both boys onto the stairs.

"Get up the stairs now, boys!"

Lindsay spun around towards the back door with the gun in her hands, not bothering to ensure that her two children complied. The retreating footsteps upwards to the second floor made it clear that there would be no more delays in their flight to safety. She brought the gun up in front of her face with two hands, pushing the barrel towards the hulking shape that was advancing on her, and squeezed the trigger.

The sound was not as loud as she'd anticipated or remembered, but she only managed to stagger the attacker, so she squeezed the trigger again. The Figure advanced on her steadily, though it was leaking blood from the shoulder and chest now. Just behind the attacker, Lindsay could see another man, similarly dressed in plain clothes and a hooded sweatshirt, stepping through the remains of the glass door. She squeezed one last time, and ran up the staircase, stumbling at the landing and turning back towards the ground floor.

"Momma, fight them!" She almost heard glee in Theo's voice, no doubt convinced that this was some interesting game. "Fight the Spacemen!"

The last shot hadn't managed to stop the advancing Spaceman. He was scrambling up the stairs on hands and knees towards Lindsay, who twisted to try and stand. While she pushed up with her knees, a strong hand grabbed her ankle and immediately pulled her towards the first floor. Lindsay's body slammed against the stairs, driving the air out of her lungs and forcing the gun from her hand. She turned her body while gasping for oxygen to see the shining orb of a face moving closer, its second hand gripping her thigh, now pulling her down.

She kicked the goo sack with her free foot, but the membrane held against the force of her kick. She kept kicking as she struggled to regain control of the pistol. The Spaceman grabbed her other leg and was now pulling her quickly towards him. Lindsay's head smacked the stairs, hard, and she twisted to grasp the gun now within her reach on the landing.

Her head smacked a stair again, sending a jolt through her jaw to the back of her eyes which were starting to go blurry. She pulled the gun around and aimed it right into the monster's face, squeezing the trigger without hesitation. Slime sprayed either wall beside the Spaceman as it fell limp on the stairs, releasing its hold on Lindsay. Before she could free herself from the stairs, however, a second monster dragged its cohort off the stairs with a quick tug then started up towards Lindsay.

With the head forced to look up at her, it was easy to take a shot that connected with the mucus sack instantly. In another spray of goo, the second creature hit the ground, but somehow there were now more appearing at the base of the stairs to clean out their comrades. Lindsay felt her heart beating rapidly in her chest. Blood was pounding in her skull and a sense of dread at her inevitable death gripped her at the sight of so many nightmare creatures pushing towards her.

With the stairway clear, another monster lurched forward, coming up the stairs with calm, plodding steps. Lindsay's hands came up, the gun level with the creature's face, and she fired. With some unknown precision that had nothing to do with speed and everything to do with timing, the monster inclined its head, avoiding the shot entirely. Panic grasped her mind tightly. All hope of fighting the creatures off to save herself and her little boys was lost.

She squeezed the trigger again, this time connecting with the star sack, crumpling another monster and forcing the rest to again clear the stairwell. Lindsay took the moment to clamber up the stairs to the landing. There was a chest of drawers along the wall, which she ran to in hopes of using it to block the stairs. She slammed her shoulder into it as her feet scrambled against the wood floor, trying to get the thing to the top of the stairs. A table lamp crashed against the floor as the dresser moved away from the wall and towards the stairs. If it wasn't for the light coming through the crack in the bathroom, the attic turned living space would have been pitch black.

The dresser teetered on the edge of the first stair for only a moment before sliding down to a stop at the landing. Footsteps on the stairs indicated there were many more Spacemen on the way. Lindsay grabbed a chair and threw it over the edge onto the staircase, then did the same with the futon mattress, although clumsily with its deadweight and floppy mass. She finally managed to heave the futon frame onto the staircase, just as hands were beginning to grab the furniture to haul it downstairs.

"Willie, open the door now!" Lindsay screamed.

With the bathroom door open, Lindsay got a good look at what was left of the small room that her father used as an additional living space/workshop for his miniatures. There were tiny pewter figures in mock battles, boxes of train track, model airplanes, and tiny jars of paint all over a very cluttered desk at the far end of the room. There on the floor beside the desk was a large metal can of paint thinner.

"Willie, grab the matches from off the toilet!"

She sprinted across the room and grabbed the jug, not waiting on her son but instead dashing back to the rail overlooking the stairwell. The monsters had made some progress with the dresser, but the pile of other furniture had slowed them down a little. Now, however, some were climbing over one another in an attempt to scale the sheer walls of the stairwell or simply clamber over the obstruction. Lindsay set the gun down to twist the top off the metal can, then immediately sloshed the liquid all over the intruders below.

Something tugged at her from behind, just as she was spilling the final remnants from the can onto the stairs below. Lindsay whirled around to see little Will's shaky hand proffering a book of matches. She didn't have to tell him to run after she snatched the matchbox. She struck one on the side of the box and dropped it onto the stairwell.

The fire broke out as quickly as she'd expected, flames chasing pools of paint thinner over bodies and debris with equal speed. Although some of them were hindered by the fires erupting on them, the Spacemen kept pushing forward. Lindsay didn't wait around long, though, sure that the old wood would soon catch flames. She picked up the pistol and made for the bathroom and her two terrified boys.

"Momma!" the boys sobbed as they ran up to grab her legs. She shut and locked the door before embracing them quickly, squatting down to their level and then pulling back.

"Boys, we have to get out of the house now. Those…"

"Spacemen."

"Spacemen, are going to be here any moment and we won't be able to fight them all. You boys are doing a great job, but we have to go out on the roof now, okay?"

She hugged them again and made for the window beside the toilet, ripping the floral curtains from the rod and flinging them away before unlocking the window and straining against it. With some unknown strength, Lindsay Macintosh managed to pry open the window, slamming the bottom half upwards with a loud thud. Without looking, she put her legs out the window and slid out and onto the roof.

"Come on boys! Hurry up!"

For the first time in their young lives, both boys complied and cooperated. Willie helped push little Theodore out the window and into Lindsay's waiting arms before clambering against the wall and out the open window himself. Behind him, the door shook with repeated blows from the mob of monsters that had made their way past the stairwell. Heat came off the house near their feet, as Lindsay hoisted Theo onto her back, his tiny arms around her neck. She held the pistol in her right hand and Will's hand in her left as she crouched low to make her way across the roof.

With careful steps, Lindsay moved as quickly as possible to the edge of the roof to try and find some way down before the fire consumed the whole house. At the apex of the first story roof, she could see a clear area off near the porch. Remembering the broken door and the gang of monsters coming through, she scanned around for a better escape route. She probably could have made it onto the garage from that distance, but the kids would never make it. Lindsay spared a glance into the bathroom, where flames spewed out of a door through which a flaming Spaceman had punched. He stumbled into the bathroom, flames engulfing him, and collapsed to his knees.

Fire clung to the creature's body and climbed its way to the head, where steam rose from the goo sack as it boiled. Boiling goo dripped from the face as flames crowned the creature and it slumped forward onto the floor. More burning monsters were coming into the bathroom then, pushing one another forward with no sense of urgency even though they were all covered in fire.

Lindsay started to panic then, fearful at the prospect of escaping the hands of murderous fiends only to be burnt alive on the roof of her father's house while clutching her children to her chest. Suddenly, as if desperation gifted her with some kind of insight, she noticed a hedge pressed up against the side of the house. Without thinking, Lindsay swung Willie up into her arms, Theo still clinging to her back like a baboon, and jumped off the house and into the bush.

Theo screamed for the second it took to drop into the bush, and pain erupted from Lindsay's face and exposed arms as the small branches and green needles scraped her. She pushed Willie out of her arms and onto the ground so that she could free herself from the tangle. Theodore maintained a death-grip on her neck, so she pried his arms apart a little to make room for air to come back.

Lindsay looked around towards the house. Flames crawled out the bathroom window upstairs and were visible inside the first level. She could see the distinct outlines of Spacemen shambling towards them from the ground floor window, so she wasted no time in grabbing Will's hand and rushing towards the minivan.

"Shit. Shit. Shit." She tried the door, but it was locked tight and the realization dawned on her then that she didn't have any way to start the vehicle anyway. Frantic, Lindsay dragged Will along behind her into the side entrance of the garage. She threw the deadbolt and pulled Theodore off her back to stand in front of her.

"Boys, you're doing great. We're going to be fine. We're going to be fine," she kept repeating as she trembled, her head darting this way and that.

Finally her eyes came to rest on the row of hooks just above the work bench on the far wall. She jogged past the old Ford Taurus station wagon over to the work bench, the boys following on her heels, and snatched a key ring from the row of hooks. She rummaged through the keys until she found the one she'd used so many times in high school to drive out to Denny's to smoke cigarettes and drink coffee.

"Come on, boys. We're leaving."

"But there's no car seat in there! It's not safe, Mommy!" whined William.

"Nothing we've done so far has been 'safe.' Just get in the car!"

She opened the door and ushered them both into the front passenger's seat before climbing into the driver's seat. Reaching across the boys, she yanked the seat belt across both of them and buckled it before doing the same for herself and inserting the key into the ignition. The engine chugged and chugged, but didn't turn over initially.

"Mommy, the car's broken."

"I love you, Theo. Please, that doesn't help."

She turned the key again, as she heard pounding at the door. Her heart thumped hard against her ribcage and her foot pumped gas while the voice of her father screamed at her 16-year-old self:

"You're going to flood it!"

The engine just chugged and chugged. The side door to the garage was rattling and giving against the force of continuous blows. Lindsay stopped, closed her eyes, and took a deep breath. She tried the key one last time and was rewarded with a loud "vroom" as the old station wagon roared to life. Theo clapped wildly while both boys cheered loudly, and Lindsay pressed the garage door opener.

They could feel the heat radiating from Lindsay's father's house, even in the garage with the door open--though it seemed that all of the creatures were focused on the side door. Lindsay mashed her foot onto the gas pedal and sped out of the garage onto the gravel driveway leading out to a chain link fence.

"Shit. Shit. Shit," she muttered as she slammed on the brakes in front of the gate. "Stay right here, boys."

Lindsay Macintosh threw open the door and ran to the gate. She could hear barking coming from behind her, but terror kept her eyes focused on getting to the gate. Her feet shuffled to a stop and she pulled the chain from around the gates, then lifted the stopping pole and shoved the gates open. When she spun around to rush back to the car, Lindsay froze in place.

The house burned bright and orange in the middle of the night, and four or five shapes shambled out of the side door towards her car. They were all on fire except for the two who had beaten a hole in the garage door only to find it empty. They dimwittedly climbed through the hole and then started walking towards the Macintosh family. Poncho Villa came limping from behind the garage, growling at the Spaceman but keeping his distance.

Lindsay whistled while running back to the car. Poncho ran as fast as he could with what looked like a couple of injured legs and a speed born of fear. She opened the rear door and Poncho jumped into the back seat of the Ford. She then slammed the door and jumped back in the driver's seat. While buckling her seat belt, she shut the door and pressed her foot down on the accelerator. The tires threw gravel behind as the car jolted forward towards the gate, a burning house bright in the rear view mirror. Lindsay gripped the wheel with both hands.

The Macintosh family bounced hard on the unpaved road, and a metallic clang came from the gate as it burst open with the force of the car. Normally a cautious driver, Lindsay stepped on the accelerator and slammed the wheel to the right as she exited the driveway. The fire was burning bright out of the passenger side window, and as she pressed the pedal harder, she spared a glance at the destruction.

The trees and garage had caught fire now, and there was a crowd of shambling monsters pouring from the back door and onto the grass, totally oblivious to the fact that they were burning. Poncho whimpered from the back seat, so Lindsay reached an arm back to pat him.

"Momma! Look out!" Willie screamed.

She slammed on the breaks as she twisted her head towards the road, her right hand still in the back seat. A horn sounded, and two bright lights blinded Lindsay as both her feet hit the brake. A hard impact brought Lindsay's head and body forward while her arm remained in the back seat, the popping and snapping sounds muted by the sound of metal crashing together. The last thing she saw as the children screamed from the passenger side was a blast of white material hitting her in the face.

15

Sitting in the front seat, not cramped in the back in his safety harness, was almost exciting enough to take William Macintosh's mind off the dull aches he was experiencing all over his body. His head hurt the worst on the side where Theo's big melon struck against his when Mommy's car smashed into Uncle Steve's big RV.

"How you doing, sport?" Uncle Steve had a weird, deep voice.

"Good. I like your big truck." Uncle Steve laughed aloud.

"Yeah? Well, good. We're almost there, little man."

They had been driving all night since running away from Grandpa's house, and now they were in the woods. The sun didn't help too much with so many trees on either side of the road, but Will could see spider webs stretching from telephone poles down to the bushes and occasionally a deer jumping between the big Christmas trees. He never would have seen that stuff from the back seat.

"I'm hungry."

"Well, we're almost there, kid. You sure you don't want to sleep?"

Uncle Steve chuckled. "Your brother is racked out back there with your mom."

"No, I want to see where we're going. Dad never lets me sit up front."

There was a wobbly wheel on the front of the car, which Uncle Steve said was from when Mommy's car hit it. Thinking about Mommy made Will's eyes hot and his head hurt even more, so he tried to find a hawk out in the woods. Will had always liked hawks and eagles because they were like airplanes. Just thinking about flying made him feel a little better, but his head hurt and he was starting to feel tired.

"Hold on, kid."

The truck lurched as Uncle Steve eased on the brakes and turned the big steering wheel to the right, taking the Macintosh family onto a dirt road leading into the woods. Uncle Steve explained to William as his mom and brother slept in the back that he was taking them to a safe place in the woods. Willie blinked hard, thinking about his mom and brother in the back of the RV on a small bed that smelled like the recycling bin back home.

William's seat squeaked and bounced as they made their way along the dirt path leading deep into the woods. The sun was up fully then, but it did little to get through the dense coverage. Occasionally, along the road, Willie caught a glimpse of a rabbit or tiny birds, but nothing as exciting as the eagle that lived near the river by his house back in Washington. He wondered what happened to his house.

Did that Godzilla get it?

Did Spacemen attack all the way up there?

Where was Dad?

"What's wrong, kid?"

William couldn't control the tears that started, nor could he control the sobs that came from thinking about his dad. He cried out loud and hid his face in his hands, embarrassed for being a crybaby but unable to stop.

"Daddy," he cried. "I want my Daddy."

Uncle Steve just sat there driving, without giving any sign that he heard or even cared. Will looked out the window to try and distract himself further, but it was no use. Mom was hurt, Dad was gone, Theo was sleeping, and Uncle Steve was too busy driving to care. Ultimately, the six-year-old ended up crying himself to sleep in the front seat of the broken RV.

***

Wind beat at his face as Will ran through an endless field of tall grass the color of the fringe along the flag that they had on display in their home. Faster and faster, Will's legs moved with such a speed that his vision blurred until the only thing visible was color: yellow on the lower half and blue above in a sky uninterrupted by clouds. The ground rapidly grew smaller as Will's blurred form parted from the confines of gravity and raised into the sky. Only an infinite field of blue existed all around William. Only a sense of incredible speed let him know that he was not staying still in that fathomless blue.

Without warning, William's forward motion stopped and a huge face appeared in front of him, zooming in from far away in space from a small point into his whole field of view. The face was wide, with deep wrinkles at the corners and flesh that looked old and spotted like Grandpa's. An enormous white beard threatened to creep all the way up to the eyes past the cheeks, and Will had to look down towards the Earth he knew to be somewhere below to find the end of such a long beard. Even with his attention pointing straight down, Will could not see the end of so much facial hair.

"Pretty big huh?" chuckled a strong voice. "Been millions of millennia in the making!" The voice laughed a huge booming laugh that made William cover his ears. Despite being loud, there was a kindness and genuine mirth to it that made Will smile and join in the raucous laughter until both were coughing, small tears forming in the corner of Wills eyes and large tears in the eyes of that giant face.

"Mr. Green," managed the voice between coughs. "You can call me Mr. Green."

"I'm William, but my mom calls me Willie."

"Oh?" asked Mr. Green with a knowing smile. "Well, William, good to meet you. Do you know why I brought you here?"

Will shook his head.

"Well, it has been an interesting day for you, hasn't it?" Will nodded and Mr. Green continued, "Are you scared?"

William's eyes grew hot with tears and his lips drew downwards into a frown, quivering slightly at the corners of his mouth. As he hung his head, the sky around them grew dark with clouds forming all around. Lightning brightened the sky in the distance and a low rumble signaled thunder on the way.

"Whoa, now. It appears that you are." The enormous face that was Mr. Green looked around at the dark clouds, made his mouth into an 'O', and began to inhale. The atmosphere began to pull into his mouth, tiny particles of cloud stuff brushing past Willie as the gloom was quickly sucked into Mr. Green's pursed lips.

"That's better." Mr. Green's smiling eyes made William feel reassured. "Things are difficult and strange right now, yes, and they will become more so quite soon. I am going to give you a gift now, yes?"

Willie's eyes grew large at the prospect of a present, but his heart was still aching for his poor mom and dad. Before he could dwell on such thoughts his hands started to itch with a strange heat. This wasn't like the time he'd reached onto the stove to grab a cookie and ended up burning the skin on his hand. This was the heat of a hug but far more strong. He held his hands up in front of his eyes, certain that he would see flames all along the skin, but there was only a faint green glow.

"Now then," the enormous face added, "your mother is going to need all the help you can give. Protect her and young…"

"Theo."

"Yes, yes. Protect her and young Theodore. Your new gift will stay with you just so long as you are a protector. Do you understand?"

Will shook his head. The sky was starting to turn a sickening shade of yellow, like the time Jimmy Cavett threw a rock at Theo and his leg bruised up. The temperature got noticeably cooler with the change in color, and Willie hugged himself to keep warm as a new wind whipped at his face.

"Finally, you must know this." Mr. Green's face was no longer jovial, his eyes tight with a grim cast and his lips straight without mirth. "Your father is dead."

Rain hit Will's head and shoulders as he shivered in the sky, staring into two gigantic eyes. He looked at his right shoulder, but instead of the dampness he'd expected, he saw small insects with thousands of legs crawling down his arms. Wherever a raindrop hit his body, a bug appeared. Frozen in horror, Will looked at the bugs that were crawling on his arms and stomach. He could feel them on his head and digging into his ears. As they nipped at his skin, Will noticed that some of the bugs wore the heads of human beings, and some wore dog heads. Each wore a different animal.

Panic filled William Macintosh as he turned away from Mr. Green to try and fly away from the terrifying creatures that were gnawing at his tiny limbs and head. His breath caught in his throat when, rather than flying, he plummeted headfirst from the sky. The sound of air rushing past his face muted his scream of fright, not only at falling headfirst into the ground, but at the cold way that he had just learned of his father's death. Will knew in his heart that Mr. Green was correct, but hearing the words made him feel small and insignificant.

The green and brown of the earth grew larger in his vision until he was almost in danger of striking it. Right before he crashed into the ground, Mr. Green's voice echoed in his ears:

"Don't open the book."

***

The seat belt stopped Will from jumping out of the passenger's seat of Uncle Steve's RV. Steve was still focused on driving along the bumpy road, and a look outside the window confirmed that they were still in the middle of the woods on their way to some place safe.

Will was wet with sweat and breathing heavily as he shuddered away the too-real dream. His hands felt warm still but he was so cold that he shivered in spite of himself, haunted by the revelation that Mr. Green had provided him.

"Did you have a good nap, kiddo?" Uncle Steve asked.

Will just sat there and shivered.

"Well, we're just about there now, so it's good you got a little rest."

Steve struggled to turn the wheel away from the damaged driver's side as they pulled into a clearing in the dense woods. The sunlight was bright in the clearing, which was as big as the park down the street from William's house. Uncle Steve parked the RV by a large rock near the edge of the trees with a bump as the vehicle lurched to a stop. After unbuckling, Steve made for the rear of the vehicle with Will following closely behind, eager to check on his mom and little brother. The cramped vehicle was littered with old beer cans, filthy plates, and boxes of cereal, but it seemed that Uncle Steve knew the location of each piece of rubbish and wound his way through the maze of clutter without pause.

On an old and beat-up mattress, covered with a sleeping bag that looked like the old Army one that Dad brought out on camping trips with Will and Theo, lay Lindsay Macintosh. Her arm was duct taped to her chest and her skin was very pale, but Steve gave Will a "thumbs up" while leaning his ear against her open mouth. Theodore was curled up near her feet, but stirred and pushed up to a sitting position when Steve moved the bed.

"Good morning, little man. Did you sleep okay?" Steve asked the groggy child.

"Good morning, Uncle Steve," Theo rubbed his eyes. "Where are we?"

"The Molalla Hills. Want to go check it out?" Theo looked down at Lindsay. "I'll look after your mom for you."

There was a moment of tension in the air as Theo stared intently at the unmoving form of his mother. Will seemed to pick up on the notion that something serious was wrong with his mother but that it was something that Steve needed the two boys gone to inspect.

"Hey, Will. Go grab some food from the fridge and take your brother outside--but stay close."

The straightforward directions reminded both boys of their dad, and they were both painfully hungry after their flight, so Theo slid over the edge of the filthy mattress and made his way to the kitchen. Uncle Steve was a slob, but the cans of Pepsi and slices of cold pizza looked safe enough, so the boys helped themselves to one of each and headed out the side door into the Molalla Hills.

16

The moment the crisp, wild air hit the boys' faces they felt instantly better. Neither one could explain why, but some combination of pine tree and dirt made them both relax. Their mom was inside the RV with Uncle Steve, who wouldn't let anything bad happen to her, and there was nothing chasing them at the moment. Overcome with an inexplicable sense of joy, the two children walked over to the rock near the front of the vehicle to eat their lunch.

Lindsay Macintosh was very conscious of what the children ingested, so part of their good mood came from the unforeseen privilege of being able to drink whole cans of Pepsi. William was quite adept at using his hands to peel back the metal tab, and was in the process of gulping down soda when his younger brother proffered a can up to him for opening. Theo clasped his hands in front of him and bounced up and down while his brother set aside his own Pepsi to do a favor for the younger Macintosh boy.

"Do you remember that statue in Nana's garden?" Theodore asked his brother. "The one with the old man in the robes with the beard?"

"Uh-uh."

"The one over by the tree with the purple flowers. The statue of the old wizard, he's got all those little animals around him and a little fire on his hand?"

"Oh! Yeah, I remember that one," William beamed after taking a bite of the cold pepperoni pizza.

Their Nana had all kinds of little statues in her house--mostly crosses, but there were wizards, too. She called them saints and got upset occasionally when Theo contended that saints are make-believe whereas wizards appear in both film and literature.

"Well his name is Mr. Brown and he visited me in my dream."

"No way!" William was taken aback. "I had a visit from a wizard too, but it was Mr. Green." He frowned then, remembering the disturbing news about their dad and the frightening way he had reentered the waking world. For a moment, both boys were silent as they chewed their food. It was as though they shared a very dark secret, one that shouldn't be spoken aloud.

The silence was interrupted only by the noise of slurping and an occasional bird call from somewhere further in the woods. Theodore was a notoriously slow eater but he gobbled down his pizza quickly, no doubt famished after a night of terrors.

"I don't believe what the wizards said," Will interrupted the contemplation. "Dad can't be dead. He was a soldier. He'll survive."

"We'll find him..." Theo stared off into the distance as if not quite believing his brother's reassurance.

Near the edge of the clearing, the bushes started to shake with movement from within. Theo's fists balled up immediately as he dropped the soda can and stood, narrowing his eyes at the shaking bush. Will stood, too, but took a step away from the motion, ready to dart towards the RV in an instant.

"RAAAARRH!" Theodore Macintosh roared at the bush with all the fury of a four-year-old dinosaur.

Slowly, the brown, furry face of a cougar emerged from the bush, treading carefully into the open. The creature was just as tall as Theo. Will's large head made him about a foot taller than the beast, but it crept towards the two as though they were dangerous. The cougar crept along softly, covering the distance between the bush and the boys in an apprehensive way that made it seem almost terrified of the two soft human children.

Will trembled behind his little brother, but Theo stared down the animal with a puffed-out chest and clenched fists, daring it to come closer with his eyes. Finally, the cougar put his haunches on the ground, curled his tail around like a house cat and stood patiently about three feet from Theodore.

"Did Mr. Brown send you?" Theo asked the wild animal.

The cougar remained still, blinking occasionally but otherwise motionless. Theo took a cautious step forward, fists still balled up as though he could punch a cougar in the eye. With the first step, the animal lowered its head slightly, even more so with the next, and by the time Theodore was within an arm's length the wild cat's head was near the ground.

Brave little Theodore unclenched his fist and brought his hand up to the animal's cheek, earning a low rumbling purr from it.

"Come on Will! He's nice!"

Seeing how tame the animal was behaving, Will hurried over beside his brother and scratched the large beast behind its ear. The cougar relaxed visibly by slumping down onto its side and the two boys spilled to the ground near it to scratch and pet its soft body.

"He's just like Ozzy!" Will exclaimed, but instantly regretted it when thoughts of his poor cat flooded his mind, filling his eyes with tears. The wild beast seemed to respond sympathetically, as it stood up and walked around Will, brushing him with enough weight to make him stagger a little.

"He IS Ozzy!" Squealed Theodore, hugging the beast before shaking it roughly. The big cat responded by nudging Theo with enough force to topple the boy, who collapsed in laughter in the middle of the clearing, grabbing at "Ozzy" and scratching his stomach.

Suddenly, the cat stopped moving and raised its large head towards the RV, as if it heard or sensed something coming. The boys looked at each other, then followed Ozzy's gaze to the trailer, expecting some kind of danger. Theo got to his feet and Will walked over to him, clasping his hand and staring at the RV expectantly.

The vehicle started to shake back and forth on its wheels and from inside a terrified scream erupted. Ozzy crouched low, muscles tense, and stared as birds flew off from the bushes at the sound of a human in agony.

"Mom," Will breathed as Theodore rushed across the clearing towards the small side door. His small hands grabbed the knob and twisted furiously at it, but it wouldn't budge. He strained against it while more screams erupted from inside. Will was shaking, tears formed at the corners of his eyes as his little brother yelled and pounded on the door.

Terrible possibilities flooded into his mind, images of Steve strangling his mom or hurting her while all he could do was stand outside and cry.

He held his hands up to his eyes, to try and hide the shame of his inability to act in that moment of panic. The tears wouldn't stop and he could feel his face getting hotter and hotter while the struggle inside grew louder. His eyes cooled instantly the moment he moved his hands.

"Enough," he said quietly.

William's hands were hot now--very hot. His fingers felt tight as he clenched them into fists. His tiny heart was beating quickly, and with each pump he could feel the blood moving into his hands, making them hotter and hotter. Theo looked back and his jaw dropped.

"Move." Theo moved out of the way just in time as Will came rushing up to the locked door. The moment his hands touched the knob, the door blew inward off its hinges--along with some of the surrounding walls--with a loud crash. Theodore just stood to the side, his mouth agape as his brother blasted a hole in the side of the vehicle.

"What the fuck!" Steve's cursing voice came from inside as his head swiveled towards the hole where the door used to be.   "Will?!?"

William Macintosh's hands were glowing a bright white, cooking the air around them as he stood on the metal steps leading into the destroyed RV.

"That's my mommy."

17

Lindsay's head lolled over to look past Steve into the gaping hole in the wall of his small RV to see a tiny silhouette standing defiantly with fists clenched at his sides. Intense light surrounded the fists and warped the air in the way pavement reflects off a desert highway. She had woken up to agony only moments earlier as Steve was doing something to her wrecked right arm, but in that moment she couldn't feel any of the pain she knew existed somewhere in the back of her mind.

"That's my mommy."

She would know that little voice anywhere, sweet little William, who woke up early every single morning to come into the bedroom and pounce on her and Pete as they clung to sleep like shipwrecked victims to flotsam. Standing there, obscured by the light streaming through the hole behind him and the white heat from his hands, she could barely comprehend that it was her son.

"Willy..." she whispered weakly as she tried to roll over towards him. Steve looked back and held her gently against the mattress.

"DON'T TOUCH HER!" Will shouted, raising his fists directly at Steve. The light seemed to intensify with the motion, causing Lindsay to squint against it. Bubbles floated behind her eyelids, but the light was so bright it shone pink through them.

"Willy, it's okay," she managed a little louder although her body was growing aware of the pain emanating from her ruined arm. He lowered his hands a little and took a tentative step forward.

"William, your mom is hurt pretty bad," began Steve. "I have to set the bones or they won't heal properly." Lindsay could hear the nervousness in his voice, like a crisis negotiator trying to talk down a psychotic holding a loaded gun.

"Mommy?"

"It's okay, son," she added to try and ease the tension. "He's helping me."

"We heard you screaming outside…" his voice trailed off and he lowered his hands back to his waist, the light fading noticeably as his hands unclenched. He shook visibly as he took small steps towards his mom, their eyes locked together.

"I know, son," Lindsay continued. "It hurts so badly, but he's right." William came close enough to rest a slightly glowing hand on her cheek. She kissed it. "I love you, baby."

"I love you too, Mom."

Theo poked his head in through the hole and pushed past the debris to his mother's side. She winced when he put his hand on her arm, but made sure to at least grit her teeth in a semblance of a smile.

"Mom, we were so worried and Mr. Brown sent Ozzy and Will blasted the door and we had Pepsi, but we thought Steve was killing you!"

Lindsay nodded along with the stream of thought, unable to interrupt even if she wanted to. Hearing her sons and knowing they were still alive and safe after the madness they'd just been through put her at ease despite the incredible pain that had fully returned. She let out a moan as her head rolled back to face the roof, but Theo didn't seem to notice and continued his rambling.

Steve was examining the remains of the side of his RV while shaking his head, but his eyes were wide with amazement at what he had just witnessed. The metal was bent and ripped inward when the door and surrounding frame slammed against the opposite wall. His kitchen was pinned underneath debris, so he tested the sheet of metal attached to the door gingerly, worried it may be hot still.

Finding it cool to the touch, Steve muscled it from off the small sink and refrigerator and pushed it back out the hole. He shoved it hard and when it fell backward onto the dirt and sparse grass, there was a cougar sitting in the middle of the clearing. They locked eyes. It looked relaxed sitting back on its haunches, but Steve maintained eye contact while edging for the pistol he kept in a cupboard above the sink.

"Boys, you need to be still," he said, keeping his eyes on the animal while cocking the weapon. "There is a cougar outside."

"Oh, that's just Ozzy." Theodore said without looking back from his mom. "Mr. Brown sent him to help us."

"What the Hell is going on?" Steve kept the weapon in his hand, ready in case the creature moved.

William came up beside Steve then and put a hand on his arm reassuringly. Immediately, Steve felt the nervous tension leave his body as though he had just gotten a massage. He looked down at the small boy with a sense of wonder and awe, inexplicably confident that even though this child had somehow blown a hole in his vehicle, everything was going to be okay.

"Okay. Ozzy? Okay." Steve was still confused, but no longer nervous. "Now that we're all acquainted, maybe we can get this whole thing figured out."

With effort, Lindsay pushed up with her left hand into a sitting position, her back against the wall. She winced at the pain in her shoulder and forearm, but Steve had managed to set the bones using wooden planks held in place with duct tape. Seeing that she was okay, Theo jumped out the hole and crossed over to Ozzy and began scratching the large cat's body. Lindsay coughed, sending pain through her chest and into her arm once more.

"Hold up, hold up," Steve said as he crossed the short distance and rummaged beneath the bed. "Let me get you something for the pain."

He produced a bottle of vodka and handed it to Lindsay, who grimaced but took it with her left hand and took a pull. She coughed a little, took another drink, then handed it back to Steve. William maneuvered around to the refrigerator and pulled another piece of pizza out before sitting on the steps to eat it.

"So, yesterday all the cell phones went dead," Lindsay began, slowly at first, talking around the pain. As the vodka did its thing, she picked up momentum, retelling in detail all that had happened in the last 24 hours. Steve could only listen, dumbfounded by the chilling events that had taken place and astounded at how easily the children had adapted to the bizarre circumstances. He asked the occasional question to clarify, especially when Lindsay recounted the abilities of the Spacemen, but mostly nodded and took the occasional drink from the glass bottle in his hand.

"Well, when our cars hit," he handed the bottle over to her when the story was complete and she gladly drank from it, this time without coughing, "that old dog broke your arm and dislocated your shoulder. Hurts like a bitch, but you'll be okay. That duct tape should keep it stable pretty well, anyhow. What I'm really wondering about is how that little kid with the pizza fuckin' went all Dragon Ball Z on my rig."

They both looked at the little boy, dangling his feet over the side of the ruined vehicle, eating cold pizza and watching his brother play with a dangerous wild animal. It was almost comical to think that just moments before this tiny little human wearing form-fitting spaceship pajamas was blasting through a door like some kind of superhuman.

"William." He looked up at the sound of his mother's voice. "William, how did you do that?"

"I don't know. My hands got all hot when I was scared for you. Mr. Green said he gave me a gift. I guess that was it."

"Mr. Green?" Steve prodded.

"He's a wizard. I think he knows Mr. Brown."

"And who is Mr. Brown?" Lindsay asked gently.

"I told you, Mom," Theo said from across the clearing. "He's the one who sent Ozzy to help us out. He's a wizard too, the one from Nana's house. The statue out back with the animals and the fire in his hand."

Lindsay and Steve exchanged a puzzled look but didn't have time to ask any more questions. Ozzy stood suddenly with his ears pinned back and slowly moved out of the clearing.

"Ozzy says we have to go, Mom," the little boy in hand-me-down Ninja Turtles jammies said as he rose to his feet. "Something bad is coming, but don't worry. Ozzy knows where to go." With that, he followed the wild cat. William swung down and walked after his brother, leaving the two adults puzzled and alone.

"Wait, stop!" Lindsay called, but neither boy showed any sign of minding. She looked at Steve, shrugged and made a motion to get up.

Steve helped Lindsay to her feet and moved to the front of the vehicle to grab a large camping backpack while she carefully made her way down, wincing with each step. He stuffed the pistol, a few boxes of ammunition, and the bottle of vodka in the already bulging pack and set it on his shoulders before grabbing a military assault rifle from behind the driver's seat and hopping onto the ground just behind Lindsay.

"Well, I can't say I approve of following two little boys and a mountain lion into the woods," Steve chuckled as they caught up with the little boys, "but as long as they're both schizophrenic, I suppose we'll be okay."

18

The path through the woods was barely bigger than most game trails, which made it perfect for a mountain lion and two little boys--not so for two full-grown adults. Lindsay was having a difficult time with the low tangle of branches that was just short enough to force her to duck. The pain from her arm was excruciating, their pace was relentless, and they had been traveling for the better part of two hours.

Ozzy seemed oblivious to his companions' needs other than to stop occasionally when he couldn't see the little boys behind him. Steve's backpack seemed full of everything, though, with plenty of water for the four of them and even some beef jerky to hold them over as they walked through the woods. The terrain was not exactly rough, but there was a definite incline, making pushing through dense foliage even more difficult.

The boys, unlike their adult companions, seemed to enjoy the outing and didn't whine at all--a fact that Lindsay found almost more annoying than the throbbing pain in her arm, since she and Pete had attempted hikes on multiple occasions with minimal success.

"How you doing?" Steve noticed that Lindsay was going much slower now that the trek had been in full swing for the majority of the morning. It was difficult to judge exactly how long they were walking, though, as the forest managed to block the sun's position overhead.

"I need to stop," Lindsay panted, struggling to push tree branches from her face with her uninjured left hand.

"That cat of his is a task master." There was a strange fondness in Steve's voice. "Just like back in the day with second platoon…"

Without warning, Lindsay bumped into William who had stopped in the middle of the trail. She staggered and grabbed a branch with her hand to stop her from trampling her son. Up ahead, Theodore was squatting low next to Ozzy's shoulder, scanning the surrounding foliage.

"Ozzy thinks we should be careful," the boy whispered back. "Mom, he knows you're tired and he thanks you for all the food. He also said he's sorry he ate the meatloaf and peed in the laundry basket. He just saw an orange cat outside is all, and he didn't want the cat thinking it could come into our house."

Lindsay's puzzlement was plain on her face, and definitely outweighed the exhaustion she felt throughout her entire body. Her son mentioned an incident that happened before he was even born, which astounded her despite having survived an attack by nightmare creatures and watching her son blast a hole in an RV with nothing more than his hands.

"Tell Ozzy--"

"He can hear you."

"Okay, Ozzy. I'll forgive the pee thing and the meatloaf, for that matter, if you let me rest a bit. Do I need to remind you of all the tuna juice you've lapped up?"

The huge mountain cat pushed past Will and Theo to brush up against Lindsay, forcing her to steady herself using the tree branch. Lindsay was amazed at how easily the human mind could accept the impossible when it presented itself as irrefutable.

This was her old cat.

Theodore could communicate with it.

Will could blast holes in things with his hands.

Seattle, and most likely Portland, had been invaded by Godzillas.

Her arm was being held together with duct tape.

"Steve, pass me the bottle."

He handed her a plastic bottle full of water.

"The other bottle."

He handed her the vodka.

The cougar returned to the head of the line, but waited patiently for Lindsay to take two long drinks and rest for a moment. An underlying sense of urgency told her that delaying their departure would prove disastrous, so she took a deep breath and nodded to Theo and Ozzy, signaling them to continue on their journey.

As the alcohol started to numb her pain, Lindsay became aware that yoga pants and a large "Moustache Cash Stash" shirt were a terrible wardrobe decision when facing an end-of-the-world scenario. She was more concerned with the little boys, traveling through the woods wearing nothing more than their pajamas. Their feet must have been made of tougher stuff than hers, since Steve was the only one in the little group wearing shoes.

Gradually, the trees thinned out around them as they made their way towards the top of the hill. The going was slightly easier for Lindsay without roots, logs and trees obscuring the path, but it began to get steeper, reminding her that she hadn't kept her New Year's Resolution.

With fewer trees, she was able to judge that it was now well past noon and the sun was beginning a rapid descent west. She was proud then that her boys were holding up as well as they were. With very little sleep they had walked for almost a full day without complaining. William was singing "Bah, Bah, Black Sheep" and Theo was practically skipping behind Ozzy.

Suddenly, Ozzy leapt off into the woods, leaving his four human companions standing in the trail, looking around in confusion. Even Theodore raised his eyebrows and shook his head as if Ozzy hadn't communicated his actions this time.

The sky was turning pink around them when they heard a crash at the base of the hill in the direction from which they left the RV. A huge flock of birds raced across the sky, doubtless frightened by the loud noise.

"We need to move," Steve said, putting shoulder under Lindsay's arm. There was an urgency in his voice that demanded action. "Quickly! We need to reach the top of the hill."

He practically dragged Lindsay up the hill towards the peak, with the two boys lagging slightly at their heels. Will looked around nervously, holding onto his little brother's hand. Without the large mountain cat to guide them, Theodore looked very frightened and small again as the weather started cooling with the approaching night.

The hilltop was nearly devoid of trees, but there were large outcroppings and a few harsh-looking bushes. Steve helped Lindsay over to a large slab of rock and got out the water, passing the bottle to the boys first. While they drank, he pulled out the pistol and checked to make sure it was loaded before handing it over to Lindsay.

"This is one of the easiest things to use--"

"I know how to use it, thanks," Lindsay interrupted his explanation. He gladly stopped talking and simply nodded his approval before setting down two full magazines on the rock next to her. He squatted down by the kids.

"Will, Theo, I want you to stay up here on the rock, okay?" He set his backpack down on the rock and pulled out a combat knife. Holding the knife in front of the children, he explained, "I'm sure you've seen one of these before, right? Well, if something bad happens to mom, like a bad man comes, Theo, I want you to just start cutting, okay?"

Theo's eyes grew large as he took the double-edged Benchmade from Uncle Steve. It was heavier than the table knives he'd used at home, and much heavier than the little pocket knife his dad let him try on sticks in the back yard.

"What about me?" Will asked, his lips quivering as he stood shaking.

A guffaw escaped Steve. "Will, you'd probably melt the damn thing!" He laughed a little more, then continued. "It's going to be your job to lift the backpack. See, it's too heavy for your scrawny little brother."

"Hey!" Theo struck a hero's pose, brandishing the knife with one hand on his hip.

Steve's laugh did not match the seriousness in his eyes, but it seemed to relax the two little boys. He replaced the water and pulled two full magazines from an outer compartment of the camping pack. After placing the magazines in his left hip pocket, Steve clicked the hard plastic buckles on the outside of the backpack, resized the straps and set it on Will's shoulders.

The weight of the backpack staggered William's small frame, but he stood straight and tall, giving a thumbs-up. Steve stood, took the assault rifle in both hands, and nodded his approval at the two children. The boys still looked nervous, but their faces showed a sense of determination with their new responsibilities.

"I don't know what's going on, but something feels off," Steve spoke to Lindsay. "I'm going to take up a position over by those bushes where I can see down the hill, okay?"

Lindsay nodded, and Steve took the pistol from her hand. He set the top part against the rock and pushed the pistol downward. With the slide stuck against the rock, the weapon was able to feed a bullet into the chamber.

"See, you can do it like that with only one hand, right?"

He handed the weapon back to her, patted her good shoulder and set off for the group of bushes that offered a view of the slope and some concealment.

Ozzy came running up the hill towards the Macintosh family, his mouth hanging open and favoring his right front paw. Theo's grip on the knife tightened and his eyes narrowed as he extended his free hand for the animal. As the cougar came up to him and the sun disappeared over the horizon, Theodore Macintosh's face took on a feral look with teeth bared and eyes squinting.

"They're coming."

19

The air grew cold with the onset of night, forcing shivers from the Macintosh family as they huddled together at the top of the hill. Ozzy took up a position on a neighboring rock formation, crouching low with a rumbling growl from deep within his chest. Steve must have been in the bushes still, although he was invisible from where the Macintoshes waited.

Somewhere down the hill, the sound of some very large thing moving in their direction made Lindsay stand up, the pain in her arm and her crippling fatigue forgotten as her body produced adrenaline. William shrunk down, crouching low amongst the stones, but Theo climbed up next to Ozzy, dagger in hand.

Squirrels, rabbits, and other small forest creatures flooded out of the bushes from down-slope, fleeing whatever terrible thing was coming. Ozzy bared his teeth, the fur on his back and neck bristling as the sound of cracking branches and trampled earth grew louder. Theo crouched low, knife held in front of his four-year-old body, while his brother covered his ears and started weeping from between the rocks.

A series of three quick pops from the bush where Steve was concealed was the only warning Lindsay had before the creature burst through the tree line about a hundred yards downhill. She tightened her grip on the pistol and squinted against the dark to get a better look at their pursuer, but from that distance she could only make out a black shadow roughly the size of their Toyota Sienna.

Three more pops sounded from Steve's rifle, then another three as the beast came closer with tremendous speed. Straining in the night's initial darkness, Lindsay was able to discern the monster's features a little more each second, although she instantly regretted the sight.

The beast resembled a bear, but with enormous arms the size of tree trunks, which were attached to paws as large as manhole covers. Whereas a normal bear would be completely covered in dark fur, this bear looked like its arms had been stretched beyond their original size and the fur was unable to remain where the skin had stretched. Indeed, even in the faint moonlight, Lindsay could see the unmistakable glistening of exposed meat and muscle tissue.

Massive shoulders extended well above the head, which was lowered for its charge. The head twitched to the side as three more pops sounded, the shots connecting with its face but not slowing it in the least. Glowing red eyes too large for the face were just above a hideously elongated snout dripping mucus. Where the upper jaw was filled with large teeth visible at that distance, the lower jaw dragged against the ground and left a furrow in the earth behind it.

"Look away!" Steve shouted from the bush, but it was too late. A flickering light appeared suddenly from just ahead of the charging monster, followed by a brilliant flash of white light that forced Lindsay's eyes away and left her blind for a moment.

With her eyes useless, she could hear rapid gunfire and a sloppy wet-sounding growl from a few yards away. She could smell burning meat and feel heat from the direction of the blast, and the growl turned into a squeal.

When she finally regained her sight, the scene before her was the most terrifying thing she had ever witnessed, let alone dreamed. The giant bear's body was burning as it stood on its hind legs. Swiping wildly at the air, it screamed in agony while its flesh cooked.

William was crouched down and shaking, a pool of urine beneath his feet, holding his knees to his chest and rocking back and forth on his heels. Theodore was still on the rock, but now held the dagger above his head, glory written on his face as he threw his head back and howled.

Ozzy shied away from the flames, seeking shelter amongst the rocks, while Steve stood in the open, taking a few more shots at the beast before dropping the magazine and replacing it with one from his pocket.

Lindsay crouched down to put her arm around Will and offer some comfort, but with the light of the burning monster, she could see human shapes coming towards them from out of the woods below.

"William," she whispered. "Willie, you're going to be okay. It's going to be okay."

She squeezed him with her good arm and he looked into her face, tears streaming from his eyes.

"Mommy, I'm scared!" His voice was weak and shaky, barely audible with his brother howling and the bear bellowing.

"I love you, son." She kissed his head then stood. She yelled to Steve, "There's more coming!"

Steve shifted the barrel of his rifle downhill, fired off a shot and froze. Even with the little light available, the Spacemen's hypnotic sacks halted his motions so that he stood transfixed. His hands went down and he dropped the rifle to the dirt, where it slid a few feet from him. The Spacemen were advancing rapidly up the hill, barely hindered by the incline or the rocks.

As Lindsay ran past the burning bear, which had fallen to its knees but still swiped at the air, Ozzy came soaring from the rocks, breaking into a run towards the coming wave of creatures. When she arrived at Steve's side, from the corner of her eye she saw young Theo running behind Ozzy, knife held above his head.

She slapped Steve on the back with the gun, yelling, "WAKE THE FUCK UP, STEVE!" before following her son down the hill into the swarm of Spacemen. Coughs and cursing from behind told her that the slap was enough to bring Steve out of his hypnosis, but she could not spare a moment of concern for the ex-soldier as she ran headlong into the chaotic scene that had enveloped young Theo.

With the hideous mucus sacks reflecting the dying light of the bear, Lindsay was able to discern her targets quite well, although her aim was not at all sufficient to the task of confronting so many at once. Her left hand was even more unaccustomed to the weight of a firearm than was her right, so the weapon shook violently as she brought it to eye level, awkwardly shutting her left eye by mistake and firing a shot that flew wildly into the night.

From up the hill she heard the sound of gunfire, and the nearest monster collapsed a mere fifty meters in front of her. More shots rang out, each followed by a slumping monster as Lindsay Macintosh stood, pistol in hand, still struggling with the concept of shooting with a hand that was unaccustomed to anything other than carrying a small child so her right hand could hold a mug of coffee.

"Theo?!?" she screamed into the night, panic exasperated by her clumsy handling of the pistol. There were more than fifty of the fiends gathering around her, and despite Steve's effort, more seemed to flood the area by the second. The smell of burning meat was still strong in her nostrils, but the light was starting to fade rapidly.

Suddenly, a monster off to her right toppled forward as it took a step, as though it tripped over something. The creatures beside it began groping towards the ground with clumsy arms, as though hunting on the forest floor for a dropped set of car keys. While the monsters to her left were dropping steadily, their lives extinguished by Steve's precision, the monsters to her right stopped their approach and began their wild groping.

Spacemen fell at an increasing rate, pausing awkwardly and then slumping to one side or another. Even sprawled as the fallen were, they still continued in their movement up the hill by crawling. Lindsay's left eye finally adjusted to the work of drawing a bead on the cosmic balloons of the fiends as they pressed forward.

Her aim had grown steadier with each shot, but improved very quickly after she stopped trying to force her hand to be steady. She simply brought the pistol towards the face of one monster, then another, until she squeezed the trigger without the accompanying pop. The slide was locked forward, which she recalled as the signal to reload, as a small amount of panic settled in the back of her mind with the never-ending ocean of monsters that threatened to sweep her up.

Shots continued from above, dropping the creatures steadily and reminding Lindsay of the instructions Steve had given her. She pressed the little button on the side of the pistol with her thumb, dropping the empty magazine into the dirt, but fear crashed over her with the realization that she left the remaining ammunition up the hill with William, Steve, and the smoldering remains of a giant bear creature.

Lindsay glimpsed Theodore rushing between Spacemen, slashing madly at their ankles with his huge combat knife. The steady look of determination on his face reminded Lindsay of when he had stubbornly insisted on setting the kitchen chair upright after knocking it over during Thanksgiving dinner. Ozzy flew out of the shadows, landing on the face of a fallen monster and slashing open the bubble until goo splashed into the air, before leaping to the next writhing creature.

Her gut instinct was to run for Theo, grab him up and flee, but something told her that he was somehow better protected with the large mountain cat in the thick of battle than he would be with her, even if both her hands were available. So, with monsters closing in on her by the second, she turned towards the top of the hill and ran. Up ahead by Steve and the rock formation where she left William, the last lights of a smoldering bear creature were starting to die down and darkness began to creep in once again. This time, the darkness was accompanied by an endless supply of demonic creatures.

Half-stumbling, Lindsay Macintosh managed to push her way to the top of the hill, where she found a smoking ruin of a corpse and her eldest son with his hands clasped over his ears. She bent down to comfort him, but was interrupted by a deafening roar from down the hill. Just then, a streak of fur shot past as a terrified mountain lion jumped on the rocks beside them.

"Mom!" Lindsay looked up to find tiny Theo on the back of the cat, breathing hard and with a terrified look in his eye. "There's another big one coming, mom! Ozzy thinks we're done for... Is he right?"

Steve dropped an empty magazine to the dirt and reloaded as he made his way over to the Macintosh family. Another roar split the night air, accompanied by the rhythmic thumping of a giant animal lumbering up the hill. Lindsay looked out into the night, which was quite well-illuminated as the moon continued its labored pace across the night sky. She saw that the seemingly endless flow of Spacemen had been reduced to perhaps two dozen, some of which were only crawling towards them since young Theo's hamstringing had left them crippled.

"I'm down to my last mag, Lindsay," Steve started but was interrupted by another ear splitting roar. Lindsay kept her gaze focused down at the incoming horde and was hypnotized by a scene of chaos she could never have imagined.

The Spacemen were only about twenty feet away, but barreling up behind them was another bear. This bear was head-and-shoulders taller than the one Steve had incinerated previously and all the more hideous, as the extra height must have come at the cost of ripping its skin and making its muscles grow far too quickly. Indeed, gore dripped from every inch of exposed flesh and only a very few patches of fur remained to cover the muscle tissue and ligaments that oozed.

The huge creature trampled crippled Spacemen in its haste up the hill, and barreled through the back ranks of standing fiends as though they were paper dolls. Bodies flew to either side as Steve dove back to the bush and opened fire with his final magazine at the charging behemoth.

Theo clung to Ozzy's back as the cat jumped from rock to rock, hissing and snarling at the monster that had finally arrived within striking distance of Lindsay and William. As the monster reared onto its hind legs, Ozzy dashed forward with Theo holding the knife point out in front of him towards the beast's legs. Lindsay slammed a magazine into the hand grip of the pistol and slammed the slide forward using the rocks like Steve had shown her what seemed a lifetime before.

The four-year-old slashed at the bear's legs as it swiped towards Lindsay and Will, but Steve's focus shifted back to the Spacemen, who were dauntless in their advance. He picked off a few more then scrambled to a position behind the rocks, keeping a rock wall between himself and the armies of the night.

Lindsay flung herself to the dirt to avoid being struck by the huge paws that slashed all around her. Pain shot through her damaged arm but she fired at the beast's face the whole time, scrambling on her back while pushing with her feet and keeping her torso centered on the mutant. She could see her tiny son dashing about between the bear's legs, using Ozzy like some kind of battle steed and staying only a few feet ahead of the swiping claws that were now focused on trying to find him.

Suddenly, a hand clamped around her ankle, squeezing with enough pressure to cause her to wince in pain, even with the persistent agony of her right arm. She turned towards her feet to see a swirling bag of cosmic goo staring at her. She turned the gun on its face and squeezed the trigger.

Panic set in as the slide locked forward with only a metallic "click". A second hand grabbed her just below her knee, its inhumanly strong thumb jabbed against her bone so hard that spasms shook her entire leg. She felt helpless with her arm duct-taped to her chest, an empty pistol, and a soulless monster using her body as a ladder. She screamed in panic as the hand at her ankle moved up to jab into her thigh with the same inhuman pressure as in her shin, but she struggled and kicked with all her energy, scrambling in the dirt with her one good hand to try and free herself from her attacker.

As she kicked and scrambled against the crippled Spaceman, Lindsay's eyes fell upon the chaotic scene that was unfolding around her. Steve was in the midst of multiple Spacemen, smashing them in what passed for their faces with the butt of his rifle. The tactic was effective in knocking down single targets, but the remaining handful of fully capable attackers were bearing down on him.

Hands grasped his arms and yanked them apart, leaving him spread-eagled and howling in pain. His arms suddenly went slack, pulled from their sockets by the terrible strength of the Spacemen and his scream intensified in the night as another one of their number grabbed his face, mashing its thumbs into his eye sockets.

Her heart dropped further as an odd illumination from the rocky outcropping showed her that the bear was still erect and swinging full force at young Theo as he clung to the mountain lion that darted between its legs. Ozzy was starting to lag though, barely avoiding the giant creature's movements as each swipe came closer to smashing into the small boy in the Ninja Turtle pajamas.

Struggling in the dirt, Lindsay Macintosh felt the monster's grip slacken suddenly as her feet connected repeatedly with its face. As she broke free and struggled to her feet, she heard a terrifying howl as Ozzy's body flew in front of her towards the rocks, knocked into the air by a final swipe from the horrible bear. Theo's tiny body rolled limply towards the rocks, coming to a halt as it collided with them.

Theo's knife landed beside her, point down in the dirt like Excalibur waiting to be pulled free. With a scream in her throat and tears in her eyes, Lindsay Macintosh grabbed the hilt with her good left hand and sprinted the short distance towards the disgusting mutant who was advancing on the spot in the rocks where William hid.

From the corner of her eye, Lindsay saw Will run over to his brother's small frame, which hadn't moved since coming to a stop against the rocks. He crouched over his brother, shaking him but receiving no response from poor Theo. As she turned her attention back to the bear, she saw from the corner of her eye a white light grow near her two boys, but her mind was consumed with revenge as she closed the few feet to the hulking mutant that was rapidly approaching her sons.

As the light grew, the bear staggered, allowing Lindsay the opportunity to stab Theo's knife deep into the beast's thigh. The unbelievably sharp knife slid in to the hilt and she tugged it down towards the earth, leaving a terrible gaping slash from mid-thigh all the way to knee. Without warning, a huge paw slammed into her, sending her flying through the night past her sons and into the dirt.

"STOP!" William's voice sounded enormous, even louder than the ringing in her ears. It pulled her momentarily from the brink of unconsciousness, forcing her eyes open against her body's desire to shut down.

William stood with his hands balled into fists and held directly in front of him, pointing towards the hideous bear-mutant which stood mere feet from him with its arms raised above its head, ready to strike. William's hands were ablaze with a light that burned Lindsay's eyes, forcing her to squint as the tears evaporated from her cheeks against the accompanying heat. The intensity of light forced the bear to stagger backwards slightly, moving its enormous paws to cover its face.

The final image burned into Lindsay's mind before her body shut down completely was her son, her little Will, standing in front of Theo's body, unleashing a blast of heat and light more brilliant than a welding torch directly into the giant mutant-bear.

20

"STOP!" William shouted past Steve's dying screams, past the dull sound of his mother's lifeless body slamming into the dirt, past Theo's limp body at his feet, past the tears in his eyes and the piss on his jammies.

To his astonishment, the nightmare creatures seemed to obey his command. The Spacemen paused from ripping apart his uncle, crushing Steve's head and wrenching the arms from their sockets, and the bear stopped only a few feet from where William stood over his brother. A thousand points of heat on his arms and hands burned bright enough to force his eyes to slits, and the heat grew so intense that he had to grit his teeth around the boiling in his veins.

With fists raised defiant at the grotesque creature threatening his brother, and tears vaporizing against his face, Will let all the fear, pain, love and heat in his body escape in an instant. White light burst from his fists into the face of the mutant, disintegrating its torso from the hips and leaving the detached arms to drop to the dirt and roll some distance.

Will shifted his fists towards the remaining creatures that had succeeded in ripping apart his uncle limb-from-limb and crushing his skull until it resembled a shriveled raisin atop his shoulders. The Spacemen vanished instantly when hit with the full force of William's righteous fury, reduced to specks of dust floating in the night air. It only took a few seconds for Will to sweep his hands across the landscape, melting any traces of their demonic presence.

The sensation of so much energy leaving his body left William unsteady, reminding him of so many sleepless nights where he woke only long enough to vomit into the bucket beside his bed while his mother rubbed his back and spoke softly to him. Indeed, as the light escaped him, it felt quite similar to any of the other natural acts of expulsion his body experienced on a daily basis.

In just a few short moments, all the torment of the last hours was gone, obliterated when William finally acted rather than huddling amongst the rocks. With his fists still glowing, Will knelt down beside his little brother and felt the tremendous guilt of knowing that he had willingly allowed his brother to be hurt so badly.

"Theo?" His voice was squeaky. "Theo, wake up."

William shook his little brother by the shoulders, exactly the same way he had on so many Saturday mornings when he wanted to watch cartoons but was still nervous about going downstairs in the dark by himself. When Theo failed to respond, William put his head down on the small child's chest, listening for a heartbeat like his father did each night before wishing them sweet dreams. There, faint but present, was a tiny heart pumping within his brother's chest. With his hands still glowing, William rubbed Theodore's chest, hoping his encouragement would help that tiny heart thump louder.

Immediately, Theo sat upright and sucked in air with an audible gasp. He sputtered and coughed as William squeezed him in a bear hug, ecstatic to have his brother alive after seeing him slam against the rocks.

"Will, you're crushing me!" Theo whispered. "Where's Mom and Ozzy?"

William looked over to his mom's body slightly downhill, new fear springing into his heart, and ran as fast as he could over the short distance. The backpack bounced against his spine as he skidded to a halt next to her unmoving form with the arm still taped against her chest and Theo's knife in her open left palm.

With bright glowing hands, he grasped his mother's head and kissed her repeatedly, whispering "Mommy" over and over as tears evaporated at the corners of his eyes. Theo was a little slower in arriving at their mother's side, but hugged her as tightly as his scrawny arms allowed. The two of them huddled over her, sobbing and weeping until the light faded from Will and was replaced with the coming dawn.

Even though Will's ability was not enough to make her wake up, when they finally stood to look at her, there was a smile on her cold lips.

21

The air was cool in the Mollala hills, just two days after the invasion of Seattle, and the Macintosh brothers shivered together as they stood over their fallen mother. A moan from near the stones at the top of the hill made them both turn to see Ozzy struggling to stand. Neither boy made a move to go to him, their bitter anguish leaving them frozen in place.

Ozzy managed to push up on shaky legs and limped over to the remains of the Macintosh family, slumping down next to Lindsay's corpse to lick her face. Theo bent down and rubbed the mountain lion, hugging the furry animal and weeping into his fur.

"He's sad," Theo broke the hours-long silence with fresh tears forming in his eyes as he translated. "He says Mom was better than most humans. Her lap was soft."

William bent down to rub the cat, too. Theo started laughing then, even as the water spilled down his cheeks.

"He says he didn't like it when she vacuumed."

Both boys started chuckling then, which led to actual laughter but did nothing to stop the tears. As the laughter faded and the tears dried, Ozzy pushed to his feet once more, only slightly steadier than before. The boys straightened with him, following him with their eyes as he limped towards the rocks.

"We have to leave," Theodore began. "Ozzy says--"

"NO!" William grabbed his mother's lifeless hand in his.

"Willie, we have to leave. This was just the beginning, and Ozzy says we need to stay alive." Will shook his head, squeezing his eyes shut against the reality of their situation. His stomach growled as if reminding him that there were other necessities that needed his attention.

Shrugging off the backpack, William dug around until he found two Cliff bars and gave one to his little brother, who took it eagerly, ripping open the package. As the boys sat in the dirt with their fallen mother, half a mutant bear, and their cat, William's fear and sorrow morphed into a sense of determination that was written on his face. Theodore could sense the change in his brother and cocked his head, trying to understand what was going on while he chewed through the energy bar.

"Ozzy is right," William's voice was steady despite the emotions circling around in his boy's body, "but I won't leave her like this."

William stood, facing down at his mother and concentrating with all of his being. His hands started glowing once again, but instead of the pain that came both times previously, only a sense of warmth flowing smoothly from his chest to his hands came this time.

He put his hands out, palms down, over his mother and allowed the warmth to flow down into his mother and the earth below her. William heard his brother gasp from behind him but continued to focus his attention into his mother, pumping more energy into her with each heartbeat. A cool glow formed underneath her skin, visible through the arms and face, as a flashlight placed in the mouth makes the skin glow.

Slowly, the heat inside her body began melting away the tape on her shoulder and the clothes on her body, revealing the shape of her glowing form. William's tears sizzled as they fell onto her frame, with her right hand over her heart and her left outstretched and pointing east. All of the terror and fear of the previous night vanished from the boys as Will's light faded, leaving their beautiful mother glowing in front of them.

William lowered his hands, and smiled as the red heat cooled quickly, leaving the loving features of his mother in smooth white stone. While her clothes and makeshift sling melted away, her hair remained, splayed around her face like a halo in white. Theo knelt beside her, stroking her cheek and kissing her forehead before standing and stepping back to stand with Ozzy. Will nodded once, then kissed his mother one last time on the mouth before retrieving the pack and knife and standing next to his brother.

Ozzy circled the boys, rubbing his body against them before padding between rocks towards the other side of the hill. With a final look over his shoulder, William left his mother on the top of an unnamed hill, memorialized in unbreakable stone with a loving smile on her lips and a hand on her heart.

22

The surviving members of the Macintosh family followed their reincarnated house cat downhill through the woods. Both wore looks of determination that would have appeared out of place on a six- and four-year-old had there been another person around to see them. They had not said a word as they followed Ozzy down the hill and into a valley with dense foliage blocking out the sky. Ozzy's steps grew steadily surer as they made their way through game trails so heavily wooded that William was forced to stoop in places, although Theo was short enough to walk through with only a slight bend in his knees.

"Ozzy says we need to remember this area," Theo broke the silence without looking back at his brother. "He says he's marked the area already, but I don't see any--oh!" Theo broke out in laughter without warning.

"What?"

"He peed all over the place!"

The boys started laughing so hard they had to stop and hold their bellies, the notion of peeing on all the trees made uproarious with the traumatic events and lack of sleep they'd just endured. Ozzy looked back at the two, cocking his head in confusion then pinning his ears back and hissing at them out of frustration before sauntering down the path.

Little Theo hugged his brother in the middle of the trail as the laughter turned to tears in both boys. They held each other for a few minutes before breaking apart.

"What are we supposed to do?" William asked his little brother. "Mom and Dad are gone now. Even Uncle Steve is gone."

"Ozzy says once we get to the…" he struggled for the word, "den! We'll be safe for a long, long time." Theo shrugged. "But he's just a cat."

On cue, Ozzy peeked from a bush and narrowed his eyes before brushing up against the two children lovingly. His status had changed upon reincarnation from one of the kids to something more of a mentor, a change that the boys found comforting now that their family was obliterated.

"It's not too much farther now," Theo said as Ozzy started down the trail again. "Just up the valley a little."

"How does Ozzy know we'll be safe there?"

"He says the area is marked too, but not with pee-pee." Theo and William both snickered. "Okay, Ozzy, we know you're serious." Ozzy swished his tail agitatedly. "He says a…wizard? Mr. Brown, maybe, marked it a long, long time ago. When we, I think he means humans, didn't have fur?" Ozzy looked back at them, still agitated. "Clothes! Are you talking about like the Indians?"

"An Indian wizard?" William was confused. "So an Indian wizard marked the den so we'll be safe there?"

"Ozzy is proud of you!"

William shook his head and continued down the trail, eager to get to their destination and off his feet. The sound of rushing water from nearby made him painfully aware of how long ago he had eaten. Apparently Theo was hungry too, as a low rumble came from his stomach up ahead.

"Ozzy, are we there yet?"

"Yeah, Ozzy are we there yet?" Theo grabbed the cat's tail. "We're getting hungry back here! We're starving!"

Ozzy turned back and hissed, but kept walking.

"Really? Awesome!"

"What did he say?"

William didn't need an answer though, as the woods suddenly gave way to a long house made of wood, nestled at the point where the two hills met. The woods were cleared in a very distinct circle around the house, which had low walls that were only slightly taller than Will on the long sides and a roof with very steep angles. The front had bright paintings in orange, red, white and black of animal paws, among other patterns.

There was only a small hole leading into the building near ground level that served as an entrance, and in the middle of the clearing directly in front of the entrance was small pool which bubbled with fresh water directly from the ground. Theo ran across, knelt down and began lapping up water alongside Ozzy. William walked slowly, a new-found sense of peace settling over him with each step as he drew closer to the spring.

Will took his place next to the mountain lion and his little brother, the cold water invigorating him as he lapped it up like an animal. He sat back after taking his fill and opened Steve's hiking backpack, pulling out the kind of Meal Ready to Eat his dad always had on their campouts. He used the combat knife to open the hard plastic and spilled the contents onto the green grass between him and his brother.

Carefully, William Macintosh cut open each pouch and the boys grabbed one apiece, eagerly wolfing down pieces of dense bread with peanut butter, chili-mac, and even some small hard cookies. Ozzy swiped the bag of chili-mac away from Theo, shooting him a look that dared him to do something about it, but Theo only raised his hands and shrugged before turning back to a pack of Skittles. The three of them sat for a moment in the fading sunlight, content after consuming enough calories between the three of them to sustain a full-grown Army Ranger.

"Ozzy says even though the monsters can't find us here, we should still stay indoors when it gets dark. He has to go hunting, though, but he'll bring us back some meat. Ozzy! We have to cook it!" Theo put his hands on his hips. "Okay, well, we'll worry about that later, then. I guess we'll have to use their fur then, won't we?"

"What's he talking about?"

"He says he used to see other two-legs--people, he means people-- eating uncooked meat and wearing fur made out of animals."

"Ozzy, I'm a big kid, but I don't know how to do that stuff."

"Ozzy says that we have plenty of time to learn."

With that, the big cat leapt away into the bushes for a night of hunting. As the sun started to sink behind the horizon and the sky grew pink, the boys both yawned deeply, exhausted from the journey and battle they had so far survived. At home they would have forced themselves to stay awake watching cartoons or getting snacks, but now they both wanted to sleep.

William gathered up the backpack and started walking with his brother, holding hands as they made their way to the small hole to investigate the great lodge. William paused at the hole and fished around in the backpack once more, this time searching for a red flashlight he'd seen earlier. He pulled it out and turned it on before shining it into the dark hole and proceeding into the longhouse.

As the light played across the dirt floors and small piles of fur bunched along the side walls, one object in particular caught William's attention. In the center of the room, something shiny reflected the glow of his flashlight. Will kept the light trained on the object as he crossed the fifteen towards it.

In the center of the room, on the dirt floor, there was a large red book lined with gold and bound with a chain.

ACT 3

23

The electronic beeps of various medical monitoring devices started from some place far away, through the black emptiness in which my numb body floated. There could be no mistake in its origin though, no dream-like misinterpretation of that incessant, skull-rending noise so I knew exactly where I was long before I made any attempt to open my eyes.

Fluorescent light streamed through the tiny gap between my eyelids, forcing them to flutter momentarily rather than obeying the signals my brain sent to them. When my eyes finally accepted their role in our mutual recovery, the only addition they provided was to replace the infinite darkness with infinite light.

Gradually, small specks of black faded into view, their edges sharpening into be the porous surface of ceiling tiles. I remember Lindsay telling me about how when Theodore was born, she stared directly into the ceiling tiles, counting the number of spots in an effort to block out the agony of him pushing into the world.

My eyes became hot with tears at the thought of Lindsay and the boys somewhere, alone in a terrifying world full of enormous, nightmare creatures, but the thought vanished as suddenly as it had appeared leaving a disgusted feeling in my mind at the callousness with which I recovered from the thought of my family.

Had I not just survived the forces of Hell in an effort to reunite with them?

"...NO RESPITE AWAITS, PEBBLE, YOUR SEED IS MINE JUST SO." The thundering, demonic voice echoed in my memory, forcing my eyes shut again as I grit my teeth.

The book.

As I lay there, just breathing with my eyes held shut, the thought of Zeke's red book filled my mind. I couldn't remember what was written in it, but for some reason the idea of blood soaking through the pages was the only concrete thought my brain would allow.

Beep...Beep...Beep.

Technology's song brought me back to reality, although the idea of that mystical tome remained in the back of my mind. With some effort, I was finally able to open my eyes completely, recognizing the familiar layout of any number of homogenized hospital rooms.

White walls, with plastic holders for charts near the door, just above the light switch.

A late model television set, suspended from the wall by a metal mounting bracket.

A computer screen, locked out from lack of use for the requisite minutes.

The metal holding half-drained sacks of IV fluid.

I was freezing there in that isolated room, with the clean walls and bright light. My muscles didn't respond when I tried to get up, causing a sense of panic to form in the pit of my stomach. The good news was that I couldn't feel a thing, but unfortunately that left me incapacitated and unable to discover where I'd ended up after my encounter with an enormous demon.

The electronic beeping must have been actively monitored though, because a brief knock at my door preceded the arrival of a middle-aged man in a lab coat. He closed the door and crossed to my bedside in a businesslike manner.

"Good morning." He put a hand on my head, looking into my eyeballs. "Do you know where you are?"

My attempt at speech amounted to a combination of moan and grunt.

"Close," he laughed. "I'm Doctor Ramirez, and you are currently in Madigan Army Medical Center."

I moaned again, my tongue felt too fat to assist in making proper words.

"You'll regain your ability to speak soon enough, don't try and rush it." He stood with arms crossed across his chest. "I'll come back in a bit to check on you. You should at least have some control over your mouth by that point. We had to put you in a coma to try and repair the damage you sustained."

With that, he turned and walked towards the door.

"I'm glad you're alive though," he said as he paused briefly at the door. "Nobody thought you'd make it this far."

"Book..." I managed weakly to his back as he shut the door, but the effort of speaking must have taxed my mind too greatly. Just as the latch clicked into place my eyes slammed shut.

The next part gets weird.

I didn't really open my eyes so much as I became conscious... kind of.

The room around me was not the same sterile white place it had been when the doc came to pay me a visit. Instead, the whole world took on an eerie grey tint, and I could see smudges all over the walls and floor. It should be noted that when I say "see" I don't mean with eyes; it's more like I could perceive everything in that room simultaneously. I could even see my own body laying there on that hospital bed, mouth open and tongue lolling stupidly.

More troubling than watching my own body breathe soundlessly from somewhere in the middle of a hospital room were the splotches that covered the walls and floor. Where the rest of the room was a subdued grey color, the splotches glowed at varying intensities of red. There were some that were so faint that they barely registered as differentiating from their grey surroundings, but some were like Darth Vader's light saber, if it was a ketchup stain.

I "moved" closer to the most vibrant splotch, a veritable atlas in electric red, which peaked out from the edges of the bed in which my body rested. The closer I got to the stain the more unnerved I became, until I was only a few inches from it, my nervousness replaced with terror strong enough to paralyze me. Sheer curiosity coupled with an abnormal inquisitiveness drove me to "touch" the thing, an action that I regret even now.

The opaque vision of a hospital room shifted quickly into the vibrant colors of reality, but rather than glimpsing the room from the comfort of my own mortal frame, I was a voyeur to a scene so real and so macabre that left no doubt as to its authenticity.

***

Doctor Ramirez stood clothed in a purple robe so dark that it resembled a starless sky. His arms extended out in a "T" like Christ on the Crucifix, but in his right hand was a black crystal about a foot long. The crystal was almost too black, as though it sucked all available light from the air, creating a void. Ramirez was chanting something in a too deep voice, his head bowed over the hospital bed directly in front of him.

Surrounding the doctor were a number of other robed and hooded figures, each with hands held above their heads and chanting in their own eerie voices. Their hands were all raised towards the center of the room, where a dark haired teenage-girl struggled against industrial strength restraints at her ankles and wrists. Her mouth was open, her scream inaudible amidst the chanting, and a white light was visible at the back of her throat.

Suddenly, Doctor Ramirez grasped the strange crystal in both hands above his head as the chant drew into a deafening crescendo. White light poured from the girl's mouth, but the crystal seemed to absorb it immediately as Ramirez raised it further above his head.

The girl's scream pierced through the noise as Ramirez brought the crystal down straight into her stomach...

***

I was thrown back into my "consciousness" although at some distance from the stain on the ground, and although my phantasmal form didn't have a stomach, I felt nauseous and repulsed nonetheless. More than nausea, I felt a sense of urgency bordering on panic at having witnessed the ritualistic killing of a girl at the hands of my caretaker. That sense of urgency also told me that returning to my corporeal form would not help me find any more information about my present position, especially since there was a fresh puddle of drool forming at the corner of my body's mouth and dribbling down my cheek.

Careful to avoid any brushes with the red stains, I moved my ghost to the door and pressed. Had I arms and legs, they would have flailed as

I stumbled through the door into a nondescript hallway connecting multiple similar rooms. Two women chatted from behind the long desk at the nurses' station, but other than the pair there was not a sign of life in the immediate area. As I moved closer to them, one shivered visibly, pausing for a moment mid-sentence before her skin emitted a faint red glow.

Instinct told me to retreat, so I backed off as the glow extended gradually to encompass the area that my ghost had previously occupied. I knew instantly that this must have been one of the cultists who participated in the barbarous killing of my room's previous occupant, so similar was the hue of her glow to the stain under my bed.

Panic gripped me quickly at the realization that one of the people responsible for killing a girl sometime in the near past was also monitoring my medical recovery, not to mention my main doctor was the one who delivered the death stroke. I retreated further down the hall, away from the nurses' station, while fighting down the dread that was rapidly consuming me.

Countless doors flew past on either side as I willed my consciousness further into the maze of hallways that made up the medical facility. My flight was erratic, driven entirely by a fear that gripped my mind even as it slept in the bed so far behind me. Occasionally, a door glowed that tell-tale red which I knew was a true indication of evil, either in the form of a past event like in my room or with the presence of some cultist.

I turned a corner to one of a million identical corridors only to find Dr. Ramirez walking directly towards me, the red tendrils streaming from him were so dark they looked almost black as they groped the walls and floor all around him. Fear gripped me then, freezing my consciousness in place while the Good Doctor drew closer, until his tendrils were almost touching what I felt was the edge of my ghost. Without thinking, I pressed against the floor.

Metal, wires, duct work, and pipes slipped past me as my incorporeal form slid through the building down towards the earth as though suddenly caught in the pull of gravity. Streaks of red indicated unbelievably strong evil presences on every floor, and it was only through sheer luck that I was able to avoid brushing up against one.

As if my ghost was bound by the laws of gravity, my downward movement suddenly stopped and I was confronted with a dimly lit room somewhere deep in the bowels of the hospital. Old gurneys and hospital equipment lined the walls, giving the impression of some kind of store room. I drifted in the dusty store room, inspecting metal shelves lined with electrical gizmos that looked like they hadn't been used since the cold war.

In my ghost form, I could feel a strange heat emanating from a wall near a particularly old looking piece of medical equipment that resembled a decompression chamber. That was the first time since entering the altered state of existence that I felt any sensation other than base emotions, primarily fear. Nothing about the warmth spoke of danger though, it was more like the warmth of a cozy blanket or a hug, inviting on a primal level.

Convinced of my own safety, I pressed against the warm wall, and found myself in a small room no bigger than a broom closet. The only piece of furniture was a gurney covered by a white sheet that concealed a very human looking form. Sitting cross-legged on top of the corpse was the opaque form of a dark haired teenage girl.

Her head turned slowly towards me as I entered the room, and somewhere inside my consciousness I heard her voice as if through a cardboard tube "Al Salaam Alaykum."

24

In the name of God, the merciful and wise, master of all things, and architect of the universe, the desert of New Mexico welcomed me with the same embrace it offered to the small lizards that scurried for the bushes as I strode past on my way north. Those tiny reptiles with their stomachs brushing against the dirt provided such irony in their cold treatment of me under God's blazing sun that I could not help but smile as I padded through the wilderness.

I focused my thoughts on each small source of life I could, pained as my idle thoughts were after so many of God's trials in such a short period of time I would not risk letting my idle mind bring doubt to His purpose. Each footfall brought me further along on my sacred quest, but the sense of urgency growing in the back of my mind told me that traveling by foot would not be sufficient to dispose of the evil that was my charge. Without a vehicle I would never make it as far as necessity dictated.

Although I was in the middle of the wilderness, I resolved to stop at the first town in my path in order to find a mode of transportation that would accommodate my journey. Staring up at the clouds and small birds that occasionally broke up the endless blue of the New Mexico sky, I had no idea how close I was to civilization. God's intervention was with me as always though, for no sooner had I cemented the notion of travel by vehicle in my mind than I noticed a break in the horizon in the form of a large billboard advertising a petroleum refueling station for large trucks.

To parallel the road that I assumed was nearby the billboard, my course needed only slight adjustment. I thanked God then for the blessings He had given me since committing myself to His divine wisdom as I walked. The providence was so uncanny that it must have been the Hand of God guiding my every step. After all, I had already survived encounters with djinn of varying ferocities, and just when I needed a little more direction, a sign had appeared to guide me on my Holy Quest. The crystal had to be destroyed.

I quickened my pace at the thought of the dark artifact that was my charge, eager to move as quickly as God would allow towards its destruction. The thought of God's providence made me think of the Blessing He had bestowed upon me, and how even after walking for so very long without rest my feet, back and entire body felt light and without any of the fatigue I had endured during physical fitness classes.

Pangs of regret and hopelessness racked me then, unbidden at the thought of my former life and the small pleasures and heartaches I had encountered in my brief existence. The pleasure of my father, God rest his soul, congratulating me when I scored remarkably in class was something I would never feel. Indeed, my pride now would only come at the behest of the Almighty for here in my new life, every moment seemed a test. The thought of my physical fitness classes did give me a different notion though, and I stopped immediately and laughed aloud as the simplicity of my revelation, no doubt another spurring from God, came fully upon me.

Taking up the stance with one foot to the rear and my hands touching the ground that I'd learned in class, I prepared myself to execute a sprint. The clean breath of the sterile desert air filled my lungs as I prayed silently , calming my mind and letting my body relax to the point that it came as an utter surprise when my muscles flared to life, propelling me forward at a rate of speed that would give Usain Bolt pause.

Trees, shrubs, dirt, and clouds all blurred by, forming into mere streaks of color like those of the stars and galaxies from Star Trek: The

Next Generation as the vessel streaked across the cosmos on the television screen while father, God rest his soul, sipped tea and smoked in the evenings. So thrilling was the sensation of moving at such a speed that I lost all track of my surroundings for the few moments of my incredible flight and soon found out that although my body healed quickly, the pain of running into a tree head-on at such speed was indeed terrible.

As I lay sprawled in the dirt with my backpack jabbing rudely into my spine as I stared into the clear expanse of New Mexico sky, my wonder at God's Divine Wisdom was all consuming. Indeed, even though my body and mostly my face were wracked with pain I could only laugh, as blood leaked from my nose and face into my mouth forcing me to sputter and cough. The coughing hurt my chest and ribs terribly, so I tried my best to slow my breathing and cease my momentary hysteria. Each cough sent a wave of agony through my body, but mostly my skull throbbed in such a way as to make me nauseous beyond control.

Gingerly, I rolled onto my side in the recovery position I'd seen depicted in numerous hospital dramas with one knee propped and my head resting on my arm. From that position, I was able to look down at my chest the rise and fall of which was in no way rhythmic or synchronized, as the left side inflated and the right could not keep pace. The collapsed lung was no doubt causing my ragged breath, but the most pain was nowhere near my chest, indeed my skull was throbbing so intensely that my vision would not remain consistent.

The fingers of my free hand lightly brushed my forehead and came back slick in front of my eyes. I prodded slightly further and where the dome of my skull was once a smooth curve, now it was wet with fluids and concave, an odd realization that was the last of my conscious thoughts.

25

"You aren't with them." the ghost-girl's voice seemed to gasp in my mind as her right hand covered lips that hadn't moved. "You're blue. Did Al Khidr send you?"

"Blue? What? Who?" I thought at her.

"It must be so," her thoughts were firm, but she didn't explain any further. "Come, if you are here then we have not a moment to lose."

She was suddenly standing beside me then, although to say beside indicates that there was some degree of distance between us when I'm not even sure that there was, and guiding me upward through the floors of the hospital. It was obvious to my consciousness that she was no novice in this ghost world, so sure were our movements through the hospital and so easily did she avoid the scattered red glows of hostile entities. Somehow, Ghost-Girl knew exactly where my body was because the trip that had taken me a lifetime of turns through the maze of hospital corridors took us a matter of moments. Soon we were back in my room hovering there above my own body which lay connected to the various monitors and IV.

"Sir," Ghost-Girl told me, "I thank you for offering to be my vessel for this endeavor, as I can only assume that you are indeed an agent of God sent to aid me in His Holy Errand."

"What? Vessel?" I thought dumbly. "What do you mean?"

There was a long pause as she seemed to digest my confusion.

"I have not adequate time to prepare you then." There was a sorrow to her thoughts that seemed as deep as if she were informing a widow of her husband's death overseas. "Shaitan is once again present on the Earth. We have been selected to stop his spreading darkness, each in our own fashion, but for you I'm afraid there is little more of a role to play than to provide me a vehicle."

"Look, Ghost-Girl," I was agitated. "If you need a car…"

"It is not an automobile that I require," her thoughts were determined but even more remorseful. "I must inhabit your body…"

Without warning, I was sucked through the strange and inexplicable space between Ghost World and the Physical World. The resulting blackness, dull pain and overall sense of fuzziness reminded me that my body was still in pretty bad shape. I struggled to open my eyes for quite some time as I was forced to deal with the reality that the same drugs that kept me from howling in agony were preventing me from even opening my eyes.

You have been drugged? Of course, they would desire to keep you still until they receive their instructions. Ghost-Girl added her own creepy commentary now from that strange, ethereal zone beyond my skin. Sir, you must allow me in while we still have a chance at escape.

FUCK OFF I thought as hard as I could in her general direction, This is my body. If you want to be useful, take a peek in the hall and let me know when they're coming.

The room grew slightly colder as I felt her presence leave the room, presumably to act as my ghostly lookout while I figured out how to break free of what I was sure was less a hospital room and more of a cell. My interaction with Ghost-Girl seemed genuine, and what I saw of Dr. Ramirez during the vision from before in my cell made me believe that this Ghost-Girl must have been his victim. If she was killed in such a bizarre and disgusting ritual, it was not very difficult to assume I would be slaughtered just as easily.

What really disturbed me about the whole thing was how everything that she had said during our brief conversation seemed to fit together with my own experience. Although the term Shaitan was new to me, I could easily assume she was referring to Satan from the Christian mythology. The notion of the existence of the Devil our Priest had always warned us about as kids gave me a chill, but it served as the most "logical" interpretation of the insane events I'd survived up to that point.

I was so convinced of Ghost-Girl's albeit brief explanation of events that should she have returned at that exact moment, I would have made every effort to send my consciousness back into Ghost World and let her drive my body wherever she wanted. Since she didn't reappear, I assumed that she was serving as my lookout so that I could find a way out of that prison on my own. One piece of information was still stuck in my mind though, cluttered amongst ideas of Satan and my own family cowering in some cave against his forces was the still vivid image of a book bound in red with gold and a chain containing it.

With more effort than it should have taken, I opened my eyes again to get another glimpse of what my environment had in store for me. My time down in the basement must have lasted much longer than I thought because there was no light spilling from the edge of the curtains covering my room's one window. The room itself was still dimly lit enough for me to notice that nothing else seemed different, indicating that no one had entered the room while I was out. An analog clock hanging on the wall told me that it was 2333 hours, which meant I had some time to escape if the drugs allowed.

Blinking my eyes worked quite well, so I tried to open my mouth.

My jaw creaked open in what must have looked like a fair imitation of the old style zombie with its lethargic movements and sloppy appearance. My tongue even lolled obligingly with its new-found freedom. With so much success, I slowly rolled my neck to the side when suddenly the room grew quite warm.

Someone is coming sir. Ghost-Girl, what a life-saver. She is red but not present.

Without a chance for me to react, the door to my room swung open to admit a middle-aged woman in a nurse's uniform. She only spared me a glance while moving purposefully towards the rack of monitors beside my bed. Signing in to the computer system only took her a moment, but she seemed agitated like I was drawing her away from something that truly mattered. Normally that type of work ethic bothered me to no end.

I mean, why the Hell did she take the job if she didn't want to check on people who had just been attacked by giant Dragons? Was her little game of Trivia Crack more important than her patient's recovery?!

This time, I was definitely fine with her distraction.

The electronic "ding" at varying decibels told me that she was adjusting the audio notifications from the computer, which would mean fewer distractions for her and more of an opportunity for me to figure out how to move my legs. Thankfully, after adjusting the monitors she retreated for the comfort of the nursing station, and I was left alone to force some movement into my fingers. With a little focus, I was even able to make a fist!

This is too slow, Sir. Ghost-Girl, so pessimistic. I believe that should you struggle for the remains of the evening, your body will still not respond to your demands. There are precious few hours until the Wizard returns, and when he does your fate will surely resemble mine own.

Damn you! I thought at her. This is my body!

I'm truly sorry for this, her thoughts touched mine. I hope that you'll forgive me.

Without further warning, my vision blurred as though Chewbacca had engaged the Hyperdrive, and I was thrown into a world of black.

26

In the name of God, the Just and Righteous, creator of eternity and Wise Counselor to His followers, the sensation of a crow ripping with his jagged beak at my face roused me from the fathomless depths of sleep. It was a continuous pinch at the flesh on my skull, an itchy and burning sensation as the beast tugged at a flap of skin near my scalp, which brought heat and tears to my eyes' edges as I brought up my hand to shoo the bird away. With a surprised squawk, the crow dropped the piece he had struggled over and took wing, leaving me once again alone in the desert.

Darkness in the desert is never as complete as one might think, for our fear as city dwellers is a loneliness that we cannot explain, but linked to our over-fondness of electricity. So was it that I sat upright and glimpsed my surroundings under the moon's pale illumination, the stars aiding little more than to act as witnesses to my strange situation.

All traces of my broken form were somehow made right as I slept through an indeterminable amount of time, but it seemed that my antagonistic crow had been supping upon my wound for some time as it was still open. I examined the edge of the wound with my finger, noting that it was quite superficial and that the crow himself must have exercised the discipline of all desert dwellers to only eat what he needed while simultaneously defending a secure source of nutrition.

Had I been a mariner of old, or perhaps one of my own desert dwelling ancestors, I would have been able to judge how long my bones had taken to knit together by the positions of celestial bodies. As it was, however, I was lost in both space and time when I stood up there in the middle of the wasteland, but I felt exceptionally light.

Suddenly, a screech that sounded only vaguely natural broke the nocturnal silence, creating a sense of dread in me that I hadn't experienced since my last encounter with the djinn. I tore the pack from my shoulders to check on the crystal, but to my horror the bag was empty, its contents strewn about the dirt where I lay only moments before. Indeed, the crystal had fallen out of the small box and was bathed in moonlight, a beacon in the darkness for all manner of devil spawn. Afraid to touch the odd glistening crystal directly, I scooped it up in a pair of pants, wrapped it, and shoved it into my backpack.

My head whipped around as another terrible screech joined the first, followed immediately by a third, then a multitude of shrill noises from the sky accompanying the dull thud of wings beating against the air. The night grew unnaturally black then, as I looked up at the moon to see it fully obscured by thousands of black shapes descending rapidly upon me from above, tiny dots of red within the mass gave me the notion that the very crow who had torn at my flesh only moments before was back to finish his meal.

The noise from above was deafening, but I knew that if I stood there any longer I'd be cut to ribbons by thousands of beaks and talons. Squatting low to retrieve my father's knives (God rest his soul), I said a brief prayer before attempting a feat for which none have prepared. I could feel the minutiae of ligaments and muscle within my thighs tighten and compress against the bone as my feet pressed deeply into the earth in preparation. It seemed as though I were moving through some viscous material as each part of me tensed, the hilts pressing into my palms such that the very metal was somehow bonded with the innumerable grooves of my hands.

When it seemed my muscles would tear against the extreme pressure, I released all of that stored energy in one enormous leap towards the swirling cacophony above my head. My fists pointed skyward with their pommels touching and blades forming an arc of silver ahead of me as my momentum took me far from the earth's surface to meet the oncoming terror. There was only silence in the infinite millisecond before I collided with the winged black cloud, but I could feel the Hand of Righteousness with me for that fraction of a heartbeat.

My knuckles collided with a wall of beaks and talons, but I felt nothing as I broke into the swarm with unthinkable momentum and spun my knives all about in an attempt to kill as many of the Corrupted as possible. The moment stretched on for years in my mind as I seemed to move with great speed while the birds still adhered to the strictures of natural law despite their unholy form. Slicing through their tiny bodies was easy enough, but there seemed a never-ending supply. Indeed, I was vaguely aware that they were clawing at my back and head as I slashed all around me to cull their number, each body almost exploding with feathers as my knives flashed a brilliant white in the swirl of red and black.

Upward momentum reversed almost imperceptibly, but I could feel the inevitable tug of gravity more than the thousand gashes across my body. The Corrupted must have sensed my shift in both attention and trajectory, because their attack intensified with beaks now thrusting towards my eyes. Forced to divert my attack towards defending my vision, the remaining beasts ripped at my torso with increased fervor, as though directed in tactics by something other than their own primitive minds.

Time became quite noticeable then, along with the pain which had been blocked previously, realizations that caused terror within me. I could spare not a moment for thought as I plummeted towards the earth in a cloud of Corrupted, my instincts were only for protecting my eyes and vital organs against the barrage. Instinct, in that case was the only thing that would keep me alive as I felt the soles of my shoes press against my feet at the initial impact with the ground.

A tremendous force was transferred through my feet and along my bones, upward towards my knees and thighs. The impact was so great that it brought my entire focus into my very bones as the energy traveled through me, the war with so many Corrupted forgotten as I existed once more beyond time. An electrical shock is the closest sensation I can attribute to the manner in which energy traversed my skeleton, but that seems a bit wrong. It was as though a car crash had occurred at my feet, but rather than crumpling my body, the whole concept that is "car crash" was transformed into a sort of electrical signal which had nowhere else to go but up.

I guided the signal along my frame, bending my knees and ankles with its passing, with an uncanny understanding of how exactly to transfer it without crumpling my body like a sack of rice. Although time didn't flow at the moment, it took every ounce of concentration I could muster to keep up with a force of nature that somehow moved faster than time itself. When the signal touched my spine, I nearly lost all control, so intricate was the microscopic system of wires making up my nervous system and so eager was the overwhelming force to follow each nerve to its tip.

Paradoxically, the gradual and instantaneously traveling energy raced through my spine, past my ribs and limbs and indeed to the base of my skull. Before it could reach my precious mind, which would have no doubt obliterated all thought from me, I threw open my mouth. In a scream that I could never have heard, all that compressed energy combined with my life's breath to create a blast that could never have been achieved through scientific means.

That lifetime within my structure was over the instant the battle cry left my lips. Corrupted dropped from the sky instantly as the energy blast entered their skulls, reverberating in nanoseconds to explode their tiny minds. I stood in a rain of feathers and corpses for only a moment before I became fully aware of myself and my surroundings.

Steady, deep breaths kept me grounded and conscious as I saw amongst the avian remains the tattered rags of my backpack. Of course, there next to the straps and buckles, pants, shirts and scraps of canvass was the iridescent glossy surface of the Damned Crystal. More alarming than the naked stone, however, was the wall of djinn moving through the desert towards me.

27

"Good morning." The words came to me through blackness so vast as to imply infinity. "Too dark? I forget eyes sometimes."

The living room was always a mess of toys, sippy cups, blankets and the occasional set of underwear or pants (kids seem to enjoy being pantless). The "L-shaped" couch was just as worn out as ever, sagging at various places and stained horribly, but it was the most welcome sight I could have imagined. I walked across the multi-colored IKEA rug of intersecting lines to plop down in the groove I'd been working on for the last seven years.

The canvas photo of Will, Theo, Lindsay, and I was exactly where I'd seen it a lifetime ago. Theo's perpetual grimace made me smile then as it did every time I looked at that picture, and Lindsay's face beamed with happiness which brought a heat to my eyes. I held my eyes shut against the oncoming tears, knowing that if I lingered too long on the kindness of Will's face that I would lose all emotional control.

"Be easy, Peter," the large voice came to me again. "His nature is why you're here."

I looked into Will's face then, his unkempt hair pushed across his large forehead, green eyes sparkling with love and joy. Tears flowed from my eyes immediately and I didn't bother containing the accompanying sobs. In that picture I saw his chubby infant hand clutching my finger, his scrunched up face as a tooth broke the gums, his ankles pointed in with his first awkward steps, the too-large Iron Man backpack he wore on the first day of Kindergarten. I could hear him calling incessantly in the night for me to comfort him from the terrors of his dreams, his small voice quivering in the darkness.

"Why?" was all I could muster through the tears.

"The most difficult question first then?" There was a humor to the voice. "Very well, the answer is a combination of genetic heritage and upbringing made your son the ideal choice to represent humanity in the coming age. Which is not to say he'll be alone. You see, linear is a completely human concept and doesn't really encompass the nature of existence, nor does the elegance of helices or the circle."

"What?" My emotional response was lost with the shift in conversation. "Look, who are you?"

"Forgive me again!" The same voice now came from the couch beside me. I turned to see an ancient man with drooping eyebrows barely concealing twinkling eyes. An incredibly white beard obscured his mouth and extended over the chest of his yellow Adidas track suit. In fact, his whole wardrobe was matching yellow and black Adidas gear with the exception of the Afghani bottle-cap hat perched back on his head.

"You can call me Uncle if you'd like. Names slip off my back so quickly since it takes a while for them to stick. When humans die, something very interesting happens. You see, a human is made up of physical material: meat bones, blood, sinew, et cetera. But there is also another bit that doesn't even belong to the physical. Have you ever known what someone else was going to say or do before they said or did it?"

"Yeah, I guess so."

"Exactly. That part knew what signal would be sent from the other person's brain to the lips, vocal chords, muscles, et cetera, to encode a message. How did you anticipate that in advance?"

"I don't know. Reading body language. Past experience in similar situations. A combination of numerous things."

"Just so. The empathy you employ or the body language reading, or whatever name you put on it all stems from the intangible bit of you that you've only borrowed. 'Soul' is the quickest way to encapsulate the concept. You grew up Catholic, think back to the lesson on the Trinity."

"Okay, God is one dude but split into three: the Father, the Son, and the Holy Ghost."

"That's right, good start. Keep that in the back of your mind. Don't worry about the whole 'in the beginning' stuff; it is not relevant to the discussion. What is relevant is that at one point, an entity split itself into 12 parts that coexist simultaneously. Two of those entities were what you'd consider lovers but a third entity was slightly jealous and wanted to be involved in the love. Now one of the lovers was completely selfless and decided that in order to make everyone content it would split itself innumerably and indefinitely. Are you with me still?"

"Guy and a chick hook up, homie is jealous so the chick blows herself to bits so that everyone gets a piece."

"Okay. Using your terminology, the Guy was still content but Homie's nature was not only jealous but manipulative. He toyed with the Chick pieces, corrupting and using them in a sort of game for his own amusement. Homie went so far as to make pieces of Chick fight and kill one another. Guy was justifiably angered by this and did his best to influence the Chick pieces to remain true to their own loving nature, but his kindness was no match for Homie's ruthlessness and corruption, so many pieces of Chick were destroyed forever."

"I'm with you, but what did Guy do?" Like an eager child at story time I edged closer to Uncle.

"He fought Homie, and as you can imagine it was a spectacular battle, very interesting to watch, but ultimately fruitless. Also quite disruptive to the Chick pieces who inevitably either chose sides or were destroyed or somehow avoided the conflict. Ultimately, however, the battle ended in a kind of draw since Homie and Guy were both of the original 12 and thus supremely powerful."

"There had to be some fallout," I said, standing up to pace the living room with one hand on my hip and the other stroking my chin. "Homie must have been furious, but what about Guy? I mean everyone has some pride. It must have killed him to see Chick hurt in all that."

"Precisely!" Uncle stood too and walked towards the kitchen. He retrieved the bottle of whisky from the freezer and a can of Sprite from the fridge, then poured equal parts into a glass. I took it from him gratefully while he continued. "Guy knew he couldn't flat-out destroy Homie, so he used his pride against him. Guy was able to convince Homie that the only way the two of them would be able to continue their relationship with Chick was to split themselves in such a way as to minimize the impact of their competition on the remainder of existence. Homie is quite intelligent, despite his terrible attitude overall (as I'm sure you're familiar with many a genius who is also a deliberate asshole), so his agreement was indeed conditional also. Are you still with me?"

"Sure."

"Okay, we have to backtrack now. Remember there were 12 originally?"

"Yeah, then one split apart and two were in some weird struggle…"

"Yes, exactly! The other nine were not idle; they just had other things going on. It's vital to look at all of the 12 as though they are a kind of family that all love each other, but as you can imagine a family of 12 will have its loners, its socialites, its jerks, its historians, et cetera."

"Uh…"

"I won't bore you with the details of all of them, but there are a few whose condition is vital to your current level of understanding. One of the Originals is the…"

It felt like a very important point he was about to make, but the combination of his soothing voice and the strong drink had the same effect on me that Lindsay's midnight talks had.

28

In the name of God, the Strength of Nations, Righteous Sword in the Night, and Bringer of Humility, the wave of Shaitan's minions brought tears to my eyes as I stood alone in the middle of the desert. My clothes were in tatters, blood leaked from my exposed flesh and I knew that somewhere near my feet was the Treacherous Nightmare Crystal which had called out for my destruction.

The image of my father's ruined body came, God rest his soul, unbidden in the face of such incredible adversity and somehow cemented my resolve. As the monsters approached from all sides, I drew in oxygen through my nose and let the life-giving force touch each cell in my body on its natural path through my body's many systems.

From the moment those first molecules passed through my nostrils, time became my ally once again. The monsters appeared to move as though underwater, each footfall labored such that they appeared almost comical in their approach. In the back of my mind I knew that mistaking these abominations as comical would lead to my downfall, so I wasted no time in closing the distance between myself and the wall of Unholy Attackers.

My feet barely touched the earth as I threw myself into the fray in less than a heartbeat, slashing two across their throats on my initial plunge. I swirled around in a tornado of metal as I sliced another's throat and plunged a dagger hilt-deep into its mucus sack face. God was truly with me then, as I lashed about in a frenzy, ensuring that each cut and jab would be fatal. I dashed between attackers, severing tendons and arteries, opening their greedy stomachs before my lungs could even complete their first inhalation.

When my lungs had reached their limit, I held my breath a moment, concentrating all the pressure within me by instinct into a kind of ball of heat in my chest. I still thrashed about on each side, striking vital organs, faces, and any body parts within my reach, while the ball grew hotter and hotter threatening to burst from my chest. Finally in a wordless yell, I spewed forth the pure energy through my lungs and out of my mouth. The energy flowed out of me in a cone from my mouth as I turned my head from side to side, catching as many monsters as possible in the cone of white heat before it tapered off.

The energy blast's intensity left me momentarily blinded, and as my vision slowly returned, I noticed that time was also returning to normal. Where there had been hundreds of monsters in my immediate vicinity, I was left alone without even their corpses to clutter the desert landscape. Whatever jubilation I felt in that moment was crushed when I heard the distinctive sound of shuffling feet across sand from behind me. As I turned, my heart sank for although I had destroyed half of the monsters with the heat wave, there were still hundreds behind me advancing steadily.

Heat crept across my skin, ignited by the rage and frustration that instantaneously replaced the inklings of fear and despair from heartbeats before. Without further thought, I raced across the desert to meet the demons head-on. My feet seemed to glide across the ground rather than making footfall, allowing me to cover the great distance in an instant.

The impact of my knives against the membranes covering the monsters' heads was negligible, and I slashed about in such a blur that my own vision was inadequate to track where exactly I struck. Necks, faces, arms, and stomachs all split as though drawing my daggers through water, but regardless of the speed with which I struck, there seemed no end to the amount of demons that encircled me.

Suddenly, a blow connected with the back of my head, staggering me forward into the flailing arms of a demon whose face I had just opened.

Just as I was recovering though, I felt impossibly strong hands grab my right arm. Reflex brought my left dagger across my chest towards where I anticipated my assailant's head would be, but before I could shake myself loose another set of hands grabbed my left wrist.

One demon pulled my right arm behind me, heedless of the natural hinge of my elbow, until I could feel the tissue connecting my forearm to my upper arm strain painfully against the pressure. As my right arm began to snap, the demons pressed my left arm against my chest and continued to push my dagger dangerously towards my ribs. With a sickening "snap", my right elbow finally succumbed to the pressure as my forearm pressed across my back. Somehow, my grip was such that the dagger remained in my hand even as the arm snapped. With pain engulfing my arm, I barely noticed as my own two daggers punctured my torso--one in the ribs on my right side, and the other deep into my back.

The agony was so profound that I was entirely unable to speak, as my arms were pinned to my body by the ungodly strength of the demons. Two sets of hands grasped my ankles, and pulled with such force that bones at my hips disconnected from their sockets. Shock must have taken over beforehand or the pain of having nearly all of my appendages broken near simultaneously would have been agonizing. As it was, however, there was so much pain throughout my body that consciousness began to fade.

"Now, now," a distinctly human voice somehow reached my ears through it all. "We must not damage her completely."

My eyes rolled back in my head, the lids flickering just enough to see the face of a middle-aged man in a lab coat.

29

The best night's sleep I'd had in my life came after I was, for all practical purposes, dead. I woke up on the couch where my family played Mario Kart together every weekend, the same couch I purchased years previous which had survived two young boys up to that point but was definitely due to be replaced. I had intended on purchasing a new couch as soon as the boys learned that a couch is neither a trampoline nor a fort, but that day was so elusive that I resigned myself to the notion that this two-piece sectional with the brown(ish) microfiber covering would be ours until the boys had graduated high school.

Lindsay would admit nothing of the sort. I always considered her ambitions for a new couch to be mundane, the sort of aspiration that was entirely materialistic and beneath her. The cushions were in decent repair, after all, and only showed a few stains that were too stubborn to succumb to the Oxiclean and steaming regimen that was a part of Lindsay's weekly routine. The frame itself was sagging a bit in the middle after repeated pile-drivers, elbow drops, frog-splashes, and front-flips.

Lindsay complained for at least 20 minutes during our whirlwind cleanup efforts preceding each barbecue or dinner party we hosted, but none of our friends were the kind to judge since the majority of them had children of their own or had watched ours grow up before their eyes.

As I sat up after that strange sleep within a dream, a terrible regret filled me. Had I told my family I loved them before sending them away so long ago? How long ago had I sent them away? Were my boys hungry or scared?

"Good morning," the old wizard in the yellow Adidas track suit said from the kitchen. His back was to me, but I could see a small bow at the base of his neck indicating he wore an apron. The smell of eggs frying and the gentle hiss of oil popping roused me from my musings. "Did you sleep well?" he asked as I stood up, stretching out the kinks where my back had conformed to the uneven surface of the couch cushions.

I made my way towards the kitchen, grunting my confirmation as I approached the coffee maker. With practiced movements, I removed the pot and put it under the tap before opening the Mr. Coffee and removing the old filter and grounds. After tossing the grounds in the trash, I replaced the filter and scooped exactly five scoops of Folgers into the new filter before shutting off the tap and filling Mr. Coffee's reservoir. How many times had I repeated these motions? I prided myself on wasting no motions during those rote activities, but had that surety of motion provided me enough spare time to spend with my family?

"Stop," my 'Uncle' said over his shoulder. "It doesn't matter how much time you wasted with your family. What matters is that you are currently wasting what precious time you have."

I took a seat in one of the tall stools at the bar attached to the sink, where I had a perfect view of Uncle's back as he pushed a spatula around in a pan. He scooped two fried eggs onto one of Lindsay's blue mix-and-match Fiesta plates and set it in front of me. He motioned for me to sit as I moved to get some silverware, then he handed me a knife and fork.

"Our little history lesson was cut short last night," he said as he rummaged through the refrigerator. "But I believe you have absorbed enough knowledge of ancient history for our purposes. The important thing is that you should recall the 12 Elder Ones are not the cohesive faction one might expect from a divine race."

After retrieving the hot sauce and sour cream from the refrigerator, Uncle placed them in front of me and brought his plate over to the bar near mine. I dressed my eggs in the usual manner, a glob of sour cream directly on top with hot sauce making what Theo described as a "volcano of red-hot lava sauce." The fried eggs were indeed perfectly cooked, salty from the oil in which they were fried, but cool from the cream with a slight zing from the hot sauce.

The flavor was good, just as I expected my eggs to taste, but there was something off about what I was doing. It was as though the eggs weren't exactly there. The consistency was right, my teeth went through them as anticipated, but when I swallowed the chewed up morsels nothing seemed to pass through my throat.

"Well that's because we aren't exactly here," Uncle said between mouthfuls of fried eggs. "I think it's about time for your next lesson, don't you?"

Despite the revelation about the incorporeal nature of my meal, I continued my methodical chewing and swallowing as he folded his hands above his plate. He stood no more than a foot away from me, but the distance between us seemed to grow impossibly. Although nothing changed about his face in terms of expression, each line, each wrinkle deepened noticeably in a way that made my guts turn. The lights dimmed around us until the bulbs no longer radiated, rather, the only light source seemed to be open flames from within the oven.

"You do indeed need to be afraid." His kind voice was unchanged but juxtaposed with the wicked lighting and fiendish visage. "You no longer exist. Your body has been taken over by a fairly misguided young human. Your wife is indeed dead, and your children no longer inhabit this plane of existence. Those cosmic entities I told you about yesterday are about to rip your entire planet and then some apart, while you drift through a shadow plane of observance.

"In fact, your id, ego, and super-ego will cease to float as they currently are. Additionally, your very protons and electrons--which would have ensured you a possibility of return given the appropriate cosmic conditions--have been altered irreparably when your body became the property of another. Indeed, you have no legacy, no physical body, nothing anchoring you to what was your world. The very soil has been salted of you."

With every word, the world grew more dismal, more hopeless. The distance between what I thought of as myself and the rest of existence grew more pronounced, leaving me with an incredible feeling of loss. I knew that he must be correct, his ominously wrinkled face with its slightly yellowed teeth and breath that smelled of old dirt cemented the hopelessness my apparitional status.

"Hope is nothing to you now." His lips didn't move, but the words echoed in what I still considered my mind, much like my encounter with the Dragon that seemed a lifetime ago. "The small bit that remains of your former being, consider it a soul, shall remain woven into the fabric of the cosmos. It will be quickly, in a cosmic sense, integrated with the aether of your medieval thought. Cling to your current notions though, 'Peter', for they will not be lost entirely."

Just as quickly as his thoughts were transferred to me, its image appeared in my consciousness. The red tome from Zeke's cabin.

"Yes, the Codex."

The thought conjured additional images: a dusty mausoleum with a forgotten king entombed, a dilapidated cabin surrounded by eerie pines, bloody faces and dismembered corpses littering a battlefield with a woman standing there holding a severed head aloft, an ancient spear covered in rust and gory remnants thrown into a ditch in a nondescript desert.

When the images faded, the imposing visage was replaced by the red leather-bound Codex.

"This will be the last remaining vestige of your previous incarnation. There will be no rebirth. The cycle is now broken for you." The book rotated before me before opening to a blank page. "This shall be your very last transaction with the inhabitants of your previous plane of existence. When your consciousness fades, imparted upon the timeless sheets before you, there will be no more 'Peter Macintosh' nor any other iteration of that selfsame being."

The dread that enveloped me at that moment was absolute, in the way that a child has no notion of dawn each evening as his parents promise there is nothing to fear from the darkness. I moved to act on Uncle's advice, intuitively transferring my experiences to the blank pages of the Codex. As the pages filled with an alien, yet vaguely familiar script, some odd sensation broke through the impending doom that had been all pervasive:

A sliver of sadistic triumph.

30

In the name of God, absent though He was, preoccupied with some other aspect of His brilliant schemes, nimbly tugging strings attached to His devoted soldiers, how faithful I remained, trapped within my own frame. It was a simple matter for me to determine that God in all His wisdom had decided I was no longer worthy of His attention. Since He gifted me with the power of deduction, and He set me on His Divine Path, why shouldn't I be able to interpret His plot as nothing more than a lark?

My solitude was complete, as was the depth of my despair, as pain greeted my body with every bump of the road. It was the excruciating pain that brought me back to consciousness, but could I have avoided returning to reality, I would have. The daggers still pinned my arms against my torso, and my legs were still folded unnaturally with my feet touching my chest. I was completely subdued by my own appendages, but as terrible as I felt--with searing pain in my ribs accompanying each breath, a constant throbbing throughout my body, and lancing spikes of agony with each jostling movement of whatever transported me--I still had some small notion of survival.

Mentally, I was still groggy and found it difficult to fully understand where I was and what was happening to me. Both apprehension and hope were eradicated from me in an instant as I attempted a deep calming breath.

My mouth was stuffed with something soft and tasted vaguely of dirt and motor fluids, which was held in place by a strip of tape across my face. Quick short breaths through my nose were all I could muster, but even those panicked breaths did little to calm me as my chest burned with heat and pain. My lungs couldn't suck air fast enough, restricted as they were with not only my arm but a dagger through each one at different angles. The healing ability seemed to allow them to inflate to a certain extent even around the silver, but something was holding my entire body in place.

I attempted to unclench my fists, hoping I could simply drop the daggers and allow some air into my lungs, but whatever was confining my chest also restricted my hands. Shallow breaths made the knives saw at my tissue, but as realization dawned on me I couldn't stifle them. The last thought that entered my mind before all faculties failed me was my entire body is mummified in duct tape.

Despite my previous triumphs and travails, I was not at all prepared for what happened once my mind ceased functioning. Indeed, the moment my head lolled forward as much as my prison allowed and my eyes flickered shut, I was suddenly free.

The sensation was disorienting at first, going from excruciating pain to lightness beyond expression startled me. The most awkward part of my new state was that I was able to perceive my current predicament in a manner of complete understanding, unfiltered by my previous senses. I could "see" my body was indeed encased in layers of duct tape and stuffed in a wooden shipping crate. My head was the only part exposed, it was slumped forward with a strip of tape across my mouth.

A faint blue outline surrounded my body, a color which I intrinsically understood as demarking the presence and type of my soul. Movement was completely different; being unhindered by my physical form, even with its enhanced capabilities, I could simply move in any direction without regard for any earthly object occupying that space.

My body was contained in a long-haul shipping truck, evidenced by its dimensions and the other similar crates. That knowledge made me quite wary of moving beyond the walls for fear that my spirit form would somehow be abandoned as my physical form continued along in the truck. I was, however quite interested in what type of monster had imprisoned me.

By willing it, I moved towards the cab of the truck and gingerly pressed the edge until I could just see into the driver's compartment. The driver wore a greasy old hat, and a Hawaiian shirt over a stained white undershirt covered his girth, but nothing about him gave off the evil that I was expecting. His spirit was not as strong as even my subdued body with its distinct blue hue, but it was indeed a slight purple like the pastel dress of a small child. I surmised that he must have been hired simply to transport a crate quickly without any knowledge of what was exactly being transported.

With no other way to improve my situation, I drifted back to the crate and arranged my spirit form on a similar crate (full of cabbages) nearby.

"Layla?" a mysterious pseudo-voice connected to me.

"Who said that?" I thought back.

"Of course you wouldn't recognize me on this plane," the air seemed to wave like when looking at where the sky meets hot pavement, and a vaguely familiar image appeared in front of me. "Surely you remember me now?"

The image was indeed familiar as al Khidr, but there was something off about him. It was as though his form had faded in color and was more orange now than the vibrant yellows of his previous visits. I felt a slight apprehension towards him for some reason instead of the elation I'd felt previously by his visits.

"No need to be nervous," he thought at me. "Being so close to the physical world must make me appear quite different to you."

"Can't you help me?"

"Straight to the point then? Very well. No, I cannot."

Although he barely paused, I could tell something was even more off than before. It was as though his features were struggling to remain constant. With each complete thought he shared with me, a strange shape seemed to peek out at the edges of his form: A shape that resembled the musculature of a large ape, but with an odd feline head.

"Since there is very little else here for you to do, until such time as your captors deliver you to whatever evil they have planned, I believe I have a worthwhile expenditure for your time."

While al Khidr's last thought formed in my mind, a large book appeared in the air before me and with it, a thought of my own. Evil.

"Now, now," al Khidr interjected. He must have somehow intuited my thoughts. "This is simply a book. It only holds the accounts of others who have fought throughout the generations. I propose that rather than sitting alone in this plane of semi-existence, waiting helplessly to watch as your body is mutilated by agents of the Devil, why not record your observations? Perhaps that would aid the next being, such as yourself, caught in a similar circumstance."

The book opened, and I did all I could to keep my thoughts private. I built a wall around my mind, around my personal thoughts, in a manner that I cannot describe. This defense was quite useful, for I could perceive in the pages of that book an odd hunger or searching. Wispy tendrils of a red so deep they could have been black emanated from the alien script of the written page--like an octopus' tentacles scan the sea floor, propelling him forward while searching for a meal.

"This timeless device," al Khidr's form wavered again, "serves as an anchor through time and space. It will allow you to communicate your experiences, but it must be filled out by you alone. I will, therefore, leave it with you, as I'm certain it shall take you some time to impart your perceptions."

With that final thought, his form faded from view, leaving only my essence and the cursed book.

31

My Dearest Love,

I love you now more than I ever let you know in life. You provided me a purpose for every trial I have ever faced. I cannot express how much you mean to me, nor can this note make up for my absence during what must have been a nightmare. I can only hope that you were able to flee with the children in time, that my premonition didn't arrive too late. Hopefully you'll never read these words, for I fear I have been deceived.

Your trust in me has never been misplaced, but I'm quite certain there is a flaw in our mutual condition as human beings. Whatever faculties we rely upon during our lives do not encompass the full extent of our potential. It is this fact that a dark entity has exploited from the dawn of time.

Why are our true capabilities suppressed? Is this some flaw in our design that limits our ability to perceive the worlds around us? Are we so dependent on our basic senses that we neglect the unseen, unsmelled, unfelt?

Remember me for my love for you, Lindsay. Remember the quiet moments we shared. Remember the joy.

My soul is doomed, condemned to these few lines in a cursed artifact that in a disgusting irony may only be understood using the finite capability of the human eye. I traded my immortal soul for the off chance that someone after me would read these words and take caution from them.

I pray, even now as I translate my essence into mere words, that whether it is you, my love, who reads this or some other member of our species, you will find some way to combat the dark force that is now part of our physical world.

It is with that spirit of love that I am able to forfeit my soul. I do this simply to provide the following warnings:

There exists a Nightmare Crystal which serves as a bridge to the world for which it is named. The crystal must be destroyed.

There is at least one Malevolent Elder One who seeks only destruction. His was the realm of dreams, and is now also the realm of man.

There are eleven Elder Ones in total, to include the Malevolent One. None can be trusted.

This book, this Void Codex, is a creation of the Elder Ones. Everything written within it has come to pass in one age or the next. Use the knowledge contained herein with care though, since a part of you will be claimed with its use.

This, unfortunately, is the extent of my warning. I hope that it will in some way help you Lindsay, or whoever is reading this, because it is all I have left to give.

If, my sweet love, you see me in this life, know that it is no longer "me". The person wearing my shape is not Pete, although I doubt you will ever meet her. She is one of the last people with any hope of returning the world to a rough semblance of peace. Her name is Layla Bashir. Help her in any way possible, as I'm certain she will be able to stop the Malevolent One.

Lindsay, I love you.

Pete

32

In the name of God, I no longer have a concept of time; nor have I a concept of space. This place in which I float is neither Heaven, nor Earth, nor even Hell.

I have poured my essence into the anchor for I know not how long. It seems I have siphoned a tremendous amount of energy though it, since recounting a memory into the anchor forces me to relive the experience for a certain amount of time. It is almost as though when I push my thoughts into the anchor, I relive the event in its entirety once more. It is for that reason that I have decided to include only the memories most pertinent to the destruction of the Nightmare Crystal, because I fear my transport is nearing its destination.

Why exactly I believe we are nearing the destination, I cannot say, just that there are numerous clues. The driver seems to stop more frequently, makes phone calls asking for directions, and there is a sort of nervous energy within him that leads me to believe that he does not enjoy this particular employer.

I have not tried to reenter my body as yet, but I can tell there is still some life remaining in it. How odd that I refer to my soul's home for all of my life as a sort of inanimate object. Yet another effect of transcribing my thoughts upon the anchor, I'm afraid. How much of my soul is left?

Going through the mind-warping experiences in detail has given me strange clarity on the nature of my Gifts, but I dare not recount them herein. Rather, suffice it to say I have merely scratched the surface of God's Gift.

"ID please." This comes from outside of the stopped truck.

"No problem," the driver's voice sounds nervous. "Got a delivery for the hospital."

"Usually those go through the logistics gate. I'm going to have to ask you to turn around."

A guard? I have never encountered a checkpoint since coming to America.

"Hold up, they said to show you this." I cannot move while scribing onto the anchor to find out what the driver is rummaging for.

"What's the hold up?" A third voice, sounds intimidating.

"This guy is trying to get to Madigan." The guard is definitely intimidated. "Sir, he had this."

What are they reviewing I'm not certain, but with the arrival of the intimidating voice, I feel a sort of heat. Not the warmth of a blanket, but of meat cooking.

"We've been waiting on this thing all week, Specialist, let him through!" The boss sounds excited, and the heat grows more intense.

"Roger, you're clear to go," the guard tells the driver. "The deliveries entrance to the hospital is clearly marked. You can't miss it."

"Thanks." The driver is obviously relieved.

As the truck pulls forward, I can feel the heat pass from the cab to the middle of the trailer, and all the way to the rear as we pass the gate. I fear something terrible is about to take place. God give me strength, I must return to my body now.

May the Peace of God be with you.

33

Little Theo,

I have only known you for the last four years, but I can tell that you and I would have gotten along quite well. It was difficult for me to relate to you for the longest time.   Did you know that? We are quite alike. It is a pity I will never get to know you as a young man, as I'm sure the two of us would be inseparable.

You know, you have this way of tilting your head to the side and raising one eyebrow when you think someone is bullshitting you. I did the same thing. I wonder if you will remember me.

You used to sing a lot. All the time, really. Small songs, silly songs, "row, row, row your butt." You replaced almost every word with "butt", and I stifled every laugh. I should have sang along with you, should have been sillier, showed you that you and I are carbon copies.

I seemed grumpy, I'm sure, but you must know that I thought I'd have more time. I didn't know the world would change so drastically. I assumed I could be hard on you, scold you, make you do chores, raise my voice because I thought I would be there with you the whole time.

First grade, middle school, high school.

I just thought that I could be hard on you early on and that later you would be able to sustain your own endeavors through hard work. It would have been easy to give you the kind of support to help you accomplish your dreams, because you would have already gone through the tough parts. Does that make sense?

Shit, if you have survived long enough to read this, you definitely have gone through the tough parts. The little boy I sent away was a caring soul, and very wild. Retain that soul.

I have one piece of advice for you, one last order:

Protect your brother.

He is older than you, bigger, and stronger, but you are tougher. You will be able to endure where he would not. He is the undying light of your mother's eye, the tenderness of heart that was rare in humanity while I walked the earth and is likely nonexistent now.

You, on the other hand, are a defender. Become hard.

It was never my hope for you to become as tough as you need to be, but I can see now that every moment I spent with you was in preparation for the nightmares that you no doubt live with.

I will love you forever,

Daddy

34

In the name of God, I will crush these demons. They have used every trick at their disposal to take over and destroy this world. They have taken my father, God rest his soul. They have ruined my body, but my spirit remains. Let this be a warning to those Djinni in the service of the Devil:

In God's Name I will eradicate you from the Earth.

Whatever your true name, djinn in al Khidr's skin, your trick has not worked. Despite your efforts I will not be trapped in this damned prison. I have successfully guarded my mind against your intrusion and will never be deceived again.

Even as I filled your pages, I retained my soul using the gift of the true Agent of God. Should any of God's children read this accursed book, take note:

Guard your thoughts, even your dreams, from the djinni who would steal your soul. Do not allow your immortal essence to be trapped within this prison, and fight with every fiber within you.

Indeed, demons of the night:
I am Layla, daughter of Bashir, and I am coming for you.

35

Sweet William,

My last thoughts are for you.

I'm not certain now how long it has been since last I saw the Earth, but I remember your face as though I saw you this morning. Your hair is messy, partially since I don't like paying for a barber, but mostly because you are constantly busy. There is no amount of gel, hairspray, or saliva that will keep your brown hair in place. You wanted a Mohawk, but I couldn't bring myself to do it.

Your eyes are brown most of the time, but there are certain days when they show the color of a fern on the side of the trail near the stream by our house. The flecks of brown always remain, too, like the spores of a fern frond. Your nose is her nose, Lindsay, your mother. Small, slightly wide, but definitely round like a cherry tomato minus the red. She gave you her looks, I gave you my weakness.

Will you ever forgive me?

I tried, Will. I really tried to make certain you wouldn't end up like me. I wanted you to go to the best schools. I would push you the whole time. Remember all those workbooks? Remember the numbers I made you write before you could touch the Nintendo? I hope you never see these words.

Your brother is going to be just fine, Will, but I know your heart. The love within you will be your undoing eventually, and I won't be there to help you rebuild like I'd always planned. This isn't a revelation for me, it's just that rather than denizens of Hell, I'd assumed life would find a way to beat against you. I'd assumed to be your counselor in those times.

Now I wish I'd taken you shooting, given you knives.

Does the world have a place for you still? Will your love and sincerity be enough? Most importantly, will you be able to comprehend when the appropriate time for violence comes?

I have a feeling that you will indeed survive, but will you be that same little boy? Will your heart remain as pure?

I shudder to imagine the world you've inherited. The pain, the agony, the fear.

These Demons work not only through their sheer savagery and physical might, but also through their ability to manipulate the human mind. I myself was tricked in such a way; the clever brutes waited until I was most vulnerable, confused and off balance. As a matter of fact, this message is the ultimate result of their trickery.

Take heart, my son, in that if you are able to read this, then there is still some hope for yourself and your brother. The other people who have been tricked into this blasphemous tome have also provided the means of salvation. Each life, each soul held herein, provides a clue in its narrative, so you must not act until you've read all of them. Most important is that of Layla Bashir, although Wulfgar should also be studied in depth for his historic value.

Layla will either walk the Earth alongside you or have recently left by the time you are able to study her story. Either way, from what I can tell she is the only one who was able to escape in time to act against the forces of whatever darkness has covered the world.

As I mentioned earlier, the artifact operates given a sacrifice. Each word you read is a sacrifice of my immortal soul, but I surmise that should you only require to read from the book you must sacrifice something from the physical realm. That is speculation, and since you are reading this currently, you must have deduced it, my clever little man!

Will, I love you so much. I'll never get to teach you to drive a stick, or throw a decent punch, or shoot a rifle, but I hope that my sacrifice was enough for you to be able to figure out those things on your own.

Things are becoming thin in this pseudo existence, Will, so I will give you my final thoughts before my soul is imprisoned in this demonic book:

I love you my son.

36

There was no way to tell whether it was old or new sweat that dripped down Private Jenkins' back underneath his body armor. Ever since the initial "invasion" some two weeks ago, all the soldiers on base were ragged. Jenkins signed up for the college money. His mother died of breast cancer when he was a freshman in high school, and from that moment on he vowed he would fight the indiscriminate killer that took so many like his precious mother.

His Armed Services Vocational Aptitude Battery scores were significant, with an overall 87 he was able to select any job from a list his recruiter gave him. After his recruiter explained all of them, Lawrence Jenkins chose X-Ray Technician, because it would give him the skills he would need later on in med school. It came with a $10,000 bonus, and his recruiter assured him he would only be working in a hospital. The thought that he was indeed working in a hospital, just not as he intended, made him chuckle.

"The fuck you laughing about?" Sergeant Withers, the short, stout veteran of the Afghanistan campaign barked at his soldier.

"Nothing, Sergeant." Jenkins still felt nervous speaking with Non-Comissioned Officers.

"Then shut up! Colonel Ramirez is the only thing keeping our asses away from those fucking monsters, so if he wants us on patrol at midnight, so be it."

"Roger, Sergeant."

Jenkins closed his mouth and watched as the numbers in the elevator slowly climbed from 1. Colonel Ramirez had selected Second Platoon for guard rotations on the research wing of the hospital some months before the invasion took place--fortunately for Jenkins--and even when all available soldiers were called on to do patrols and raids toward the city, the Colonel retained his guard force.

As the numbers ticked up, Jenkins couldn't help but wonder how he got so lucky. During his shifts since the invasion, he had seen a good number of soldiers come back mangled--bits of their arms ripped apart, gaping wounds in their abdomens, legs bent in impossible angles. The thing that made him sweat tonight, though, was the most recent group being treated in the Emergency section.

For the past few days, Jenkins had noticed a disturbing number of soldiers brought in for treatment with identical injuries. All of them had their eyes gouged out, with rake marks from their eye sockets across their cheeks. At first, it seemed as though the demons had adopted a new tactic, a way to circumvent the body armor and helmets--a notion that seemed easy to accept from an outside perspective. After the first day of seeing soldier after soldier treated for the same injuries, however, Jenkins began to wonder.

The young private felt a macabre sense of shame for admitting it, even within his own thoughts, but the very first thing that made him think something was amiss had to do with the ludicrous concerns the Army places upon eye protection. The old joke around the barracks was that with a reflective belt and a pair of goggles, a soldier was invincible. With all the emphasis on ballistic glasses, how would any enemy be able to circumvent that simple defensive posture?

The most telling sign, however, came the following day during Jenkins' shift, when he happened to see yet another victim of the gruesome tactic. His head was shaking as he lay on the stretcher in the hall awaiting treatment, and his body was covered with a silver heat blanket. As Jenkins walked by, the poor soul's hand slipped from beneath the blanket, shaking and dripping fresh blood.

Jenkins shuddered at the memory and the terrible conclusion he had drawn at that moment. These soldiers had torn their own eyes out.

Numbers clicked too slowly as Jenkins stared at the distinct red numerals next to the illuminated "up" arrow. 5, 6, 7, and 8 all clicked by at the normal interval, but when the elevator continued towards their destination, it seemed to struggle. Jenkins held his gaze on those glowing red digits, anticipating the number 9 to show like it had every night for the past months. His heart, pounded against his ribs, as if trying to free itself, and his eyes refused to blink.

He turned to Sergeant Withers, but that simple motion required all of his concentration, the entirety of his consciousness. It was like turning his head through some viscous fluid. As his head lolled to the side, an elongated "ding" resonated for what seemed an eternity. Private Jenkins felt the vibrations on every hair through his ear canal as it shook the membrane. When his brain finally interpreted the sensation as relating to the elevator, the moment was finished. That strange moment of clarity disappeared immediately as Jenkins turned his head back just in time to see the doors part in the middle, oddly punctuated by the routine humming of gears as the doors slid into place.

"All available security personnel!" The female voice sounded panicked over the intercom. "Proceed to the--"

The young soldier stared dumbly down the hall as a man in a hospital gown held a nurse by the throat. Her hands dropped the microphone as they reached for the man's arm, ending the attempted distress call while broadcasting her final gurgling cough as the man squeezed her larynx.

Fear gripped Jenkins to the core, freezing him in place as he watched Sergeant Withers dash towards the man. Withers shouted something as he raised his rifle towards the deranged patient, but it was too late. There was a crunching, wet sound as the man slammed his free fist into the nurse's face so hard that it seemed to bypass her nose entirely and embed itself into her skull. Gore flew from the hole in the woman's face as the man wrenched his fist free, splashing the hallway in blood and grey matter.

As hot urine soaked Jenkins' pants, he clasped his hands over his ears at the sound of Withers' rifle firing, but somehow the man was faster. In a blur, he closed the distance to the Non-Commissioned Officer, miraculously avoiding the spray of hot lead that flew past him into the nurses' station. The man was simply there alongside Withers, with one hand on the rifle and the other striking the soldier with a palm-heel to the temple.

The mechanical "ding" barely registered in Jenkins' mind as the doors slid shut at a snail's pace. All he could do was watch his squad leader's corpse slump against the wall while the lunatic tossed the rifle aside as though it were useless. The man dashed in the opposite direction as the doors blocked the horrible scene, leaving Jenkins alone in the elevator. Tears streamed down his cheeks and his legs gave out beneath him, leaving the young soldier shaking on the floor in a puddle of his own piss.

37

"Sir, there's an emergency at the hospital." The soldier was out of breath, as though he had run the three miles from the hospital to the dilapidated house in the middle of the woods that served as a secure research facility. Situated in a clearing deep within the woods, the two-story facility was a house in outer appearance only. Three of the four rooms on the first floor were filled to the ceiling in bookshelves, each completely full of ancient texts and occasionally a small trophy or oddity behind a display glass. A rust-covered watch. A skeletal hand that was only vaguely human. The skull of a tusked animal. A pair of silver daggers. Mismatched seats and Army field tables were the only furniture, but in what had been originally been intended as a parlor or dining room was a long table with computers and communications equipment.

Seated in a high-backed leather chair, a man in his late forties looked up from a diagram of some kind to stare into the young soldier's face.

"What is the emergency, boy?" the stern voice spat.

"Doctor Ramirez, one of your patients…"

The soldier continued speaking, but the doctor's eyes had rolled into the back of his skull. His mouth opened and shut without a sound as the soldier continued his story. Whether or not the doctor heard, it seemed that the soldier would spare no details. Before the enlisted man finished his report, the doctor's eyes blinked back to normal.

Suddenly, the doctor was on his feet, pushing aside the bewildered soldier and racing towards the kitchen to the rear of the house. Near the refrigerator there was a door which was both bolted and locked. In front of it, Doctor Ramirez fumbled in the pockets of his cargo pants as sweat began pouring down his neck, cheeks, and forehead.

The sound of gunfire nearby made him jerk his head towards the main entrance to the cabin, but he knew there was no amount of gunfire, no amount of soldiers that could halt this particular enemy's advance. With a shaky hand, Doctor Ramirez unlocked the handle, slid open the deadbolt, and rushed down the stairs.

His heart beat against his chest as he descended the short flight to the dimly lit basement. There were four pillars in the center of the open room, with a heating system located just behind the staircase, but the only noticeable object was a small metal container about a foot long and only a few inches wide, like some inexplicably ornate pencil case. Shadows danced along the concrete as Doctor Ramirez rushed to the center of the room, upsetting the lines of candles which were the only source of light.

Gunshots and shouting just outside the front door forced him to hurry, so the doctor began mumbling to himself as he pulled a small box from his right cargo pocket. He pulled out a cylindrical piece of chalk, and wasting no time started marking the floor around the intricate box on the ground. The pattern was a simple one to him, as though he had practiced it enough that it was now a matter of muscle memory. Straight lines first, then curves, all the while mumbling some bizarre incantation.

"Stop or I'll--" The soldier from earlier failed deliver his second message of the night as his body thumped onto the floor above.

"You're too late!" Doctor Ramirez shouted triumphantly as he stood facing the staircase. His legs straddled the box. "I've killed you once already! Doing so a second time will be as simple. This time, however, I doubt you'll be able to return."

The silhouette at the top of the stair did not pause at the confident taunts of the doctor. As the shape descended, however, Ramirez grew pale as a strange recognition came over him.

"You," the doctor stammered. "How…?"

The man standing at the base of the stairs was of average height, with short brown hair and an unkempt growth of beard indicating weeks in the field. His body was covered in a tattered, blood-soaked hospital gown and his shoulders moved up and down with each breath.

"Pimp!" The word came out awkwardly from the deranged patient, and the look of surprise on his face mirrored that of the doctor's. It was as though the man was surprised by his own words. "Son of a whore! In the name of God, your corruption ends this night!"

As he took a step towards the doctor, his foot stopped just at the edge of the hastily drawn geometric pattern on the floor. Sweat continued to pour from Doctor Ramirez's forehead and his eyes went wide as the man lifted his foot to take another step.

The moment his foot crossed over the strange shapes on the grown, the man stopped. He looked around puzzled and struggled to lift his legs. Doctor Ramirez's face split open in a wicked grin, and he threw his head back with uproarious laughter.

"Amateur!" He cackled while the man continued his struggle against invisible bonds. "You are as lost as the Arab bitch! Do you even realize what I've done? You're trapped, you fool! I've won!"

"How?"

"Irrelevant! And do you know who did nothing to stop me? Your 'God'!" The doctor was shaking with sadistic delight as he approached his frozen victim. "Even those fucking idiots guarding their sacred stone in the desert had no idea what was going on, not until it was too late! For a thousand years those idiots touched their heads to the sand, ignorant of what the they were guarding! They didn't even realize they were guarding anything--not until I killed their puppet to open the Seals!"

Doctor Ramirez was close enough to stroke the man's chin and pinch his cheeks like a child. "No, she posed no problem at all. Can you imagine if they actually realized what they bowed to five times a day? If they really and truly understood what was hiding under that big black box in the desert?"

The doctor bent down to retrieve the box from the floor, slapping it across the man's face. As the metal touched his skin, the man's eyes went entirely white. The doctor took one step backward, still clutching the box, but where there was gloating triumph a moment before a small sensation of fear was visible at the corner of his eyes.

Suddenly, the man inhaled, drawing in all the light from the candles and the light spilling from the top of the stairs with the oxygen from the room. The basement was plunged into darkness so complete that

Doctor Ramirez began to shake once more.

"I am an instrument of darkness!" The quiver in his voice exposed his lie "What use is…"

His voice trailed off as two white orbs appeared in front of him. Ramirez had spent the majority of his years, even as a child, devoted to the Black Arts. Blood rituals, curses, and all manner of evil instruments were his specialty. He had gone into medicine with the intention of mastering all manner of controlling human beings, to learn every way to gain power over them. With all of his terrible knowledge--and even with his recent success with the Seals--he was unable to fathom what this man was attempting.

Another light appeared, opening slowly just below the two eyes and Ramirez understood it to be the man's mouth opening.

"You have betrayed your very species." The intense light blinked on and off as his mouth formed the words. "You have desecrated our sacred place in your quest for power. And you have killed my father, God rest his soul."

With the last word, the light grew suddenly more intense, as though a small sun was exploding in the basement. The doctor slammed his eyes shut and threw his hands up to block out the light, but it couldn't help. Heat started over every inch of his skin. Like the sun at noon at first, but with each passing moment it became more and more painful. The heat of the sun turned into the heat of fire, and Doctor Ramirez could smell his flesh cooking slowly. He threw his head back and screamed. Even beyond his skin roasting, Doctor Ramirez experienced a hand grabbing his wrist while another pried the box from his grasp.

"My name is Layla, daughter of Bashir, and it is in the name of God that I eradicate you from His Earth."

ABOUT THE AUTHOR

Isaiah Creel is an Army Linguist, Afghan campaign veteran, and father of three. He considers the Pacific Northwest home, but he has lived in various places throughout the United States.